I0762066

RUINED WINGS

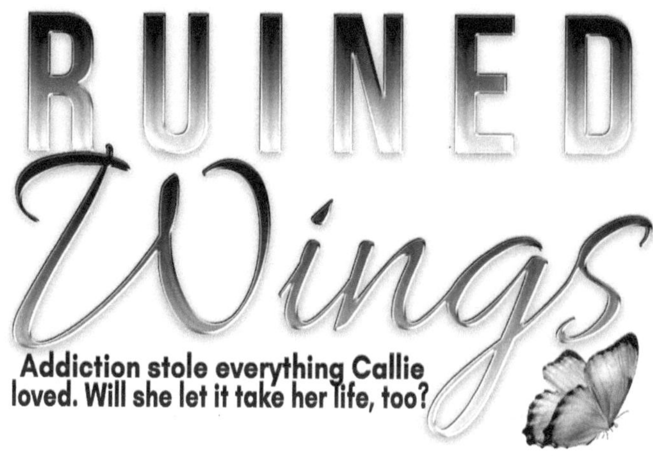

ASHLEY FONTAINNE

Cover and Interior book design by One of a Kind Covers

RUINED WINGS

Hardcover Published by MPI Publishing

ISBN 13: 978-0-9960179-5-4

Contents

OTHER BOOKS BY ASHLEY FONTAINNE

The Rememdium Series/Sci-fi/Post-Apocalyptic:
Tainted Cure – Book 1
Tainted Reality – Book 2
Tainted Future – Book 3
Tainted World – Book 4 (coming soon)

The Magnolia Series (written with Lillian Hansen):
Blood Ties
Blood Loss (coming soon)
Blood Stain (coming soon)

Mystery/suspense novels:
Night Court
Whispered Pain
Empty Shell
Suicide Lake
Number Seventy-Five – soon to be a feature film
http://www.number75themovie.com

Eviscerating the Snake Trilogy:
Accountable to None
Zero Balance
Adjusting Journal Entries

Paranormal/suspense:
Growl
The Lie – soon to be the feature film *Foreseen*
http://www.foreseenmovie.com

Dark Comedy:
Suburbia Made Me Do It (coming soon)

Poetry and Short Stories:
Fine as Frog Hair

Ramblings of a Mad Southern Woman

Stay up to date with new releases, movie news, and more! Sign up for
Ashley's newsletter on her website at
http://www.ashleyfontainne.com

1

CHAPTER ONE

Three Years Ago

"Novak! Stop pacing! You're using too much energy before the final race!"

Callie Novak winced at Coach Patterson's words yet didn't stop moving. Somehow the sensation of the cleats clicking on the pavement gave her a sense of balance. Nervous energy thrummed throughout her body, which wasn't unusual before a big meet. The unusual part was the heaviness in her legs, back, and chest. She continued pacing, sweat dripping down her brow and back. Callie wondered if she was having a panic attack or something similar. She'd seen her mother and brother suffer bouts of anxiety over the years. Did she inherit the trait too? No, the stress and strain was normal since Callie's entire future was riding on her performance tonight in the final of the Women's 1600.

"Novak, did you hear me?" Coach Patterson barked, coming up behind his star athlete. He touched her shoulder and felt the dampness. "Okay, CeeCee. What's wrong? Did you pull something in the last heat? I've never seen you so stressed out."

Sighing, Callie turned to face her coach. He was one of the few people other than her immediate family who called her by the quirky nickname. Coach Patterson looked jittery, his face flushed and smile fake. They both were antsy. It was the last meet of the year, and rumors tore through the school the entire week, spreading fast about the possibility of scouts from U of A, UALR, LSU, and other colleges in the stands. If Callie could shave just a few seconds from her usual time, she'd be a shoe-in for scholarships to the schools.

Another rumor was Coach Patterson had been promised a huge raise by the school district if Callie signed with the Razorbacks. *No pressure at all* Callie thought. "No, I'm fine. I just…I hate starting a final race without a good luck hug from my dad and Colton."

"They're just stuck in traffic like everyone else. Look at the stands. They're practically empty! You know they're both irritated they got held up by the accident on 40. Come on now, breathe. Focus. You've trained hard for months; don't lose your edge by worrying about things you can't control. Warrior mind and body, remember?"

Biting her lip to keep from saying a nasty comment out loud about Coach P's obsession with the weird phrase, Callie simply nodded.

"Besides," Coach Patterson continued, "when you make it to college after next year, they won't be able to attend all your meets out of state."

"Colton will be going to Fayetteville, too," Callie interrupted, "if I get in on a free ride. He'll come with me…. I guarantee you he'll find a way, even if it means being water boy or toting towels."

Coach Patterson gave Callie a stern look. "You need to learn to rely on your own inner strength to win, Novak. Pull from what's inside you, not around you. You're one tough and determined girl, though sometimes I think you forget that."

Chuckling, Callie gave her mentor a weary smile. "And sometimes you forget I just turned seventeen. A lot is riding on my shoulders."

"You're right, but only because you decided to pick up a ton of responsibility that wasn't yours to carry. Novak, win this race for you and no one else. Not your dad, mom, brother, boyfriend, friends, teammates, or even me. This is *your* time to shine. The rest of us just get to bask in the glowing rays of your success. Now, shake off the worries about everything, including who may or may not be in the stands watching. Focus on giving everything you've got to the race. For you."

"You're right, as always." Callie smiled while glancing back one more time to the stands. Kevin and her mom were each grinning widely as they held signs over their heads reading *Go, CeeCee, Go!* "I'm sure my dad's dropped plenty of f-bombs. Maybe slammed his fist on the dash a few times, too. Poor Colton is probably cringing at this point. He hates it when Dad gets all fired up and starts cussing."

Following her gaze, Coach Patterson gave Callie a gentle push forward. "Why don't you go get an extra hug from your mom and Kevin then come back and stretch?"

Nodding once in agreement, Callie jogged to the stands. Her

mother smiled and waved, but the overwhelming sense of dread still hung heavy over Callie's mind even after receiving a warm hug from her mom and boyfriend.

"Have you heard from Dad or Colton? Are they close?" Callie asked after brushing a light kiss on Kevin's cheek.

A shadow of irritation flickered behind her mother's blue eyes. "My cell's dead, so no. Don't worry, baby. I did remember to charge the video camera, so even if they miss it, they'll be able to watch you run to victory later!"

Callie shook her legs to rid them of the heaviness, which increased after the short jog.

"Muscle cramps?"

"No, Mom. Something else—something I've never felt before," Callie grumbled, slapping her thighs to wake them up. "Just my nerves I guess. Last race of my junior year—guess it's more important to me than I realized. Kevin? Do you have your phone?"

Shaking a mop of thick mahogany hair, Kevin replied, "Nope. Don't you remember the warning you gave me last time I brought it?"

Smiling, Callie remarked, "Oops, forgot I threatened to smash it to pieces if you didn't quit posting live video feeds of me on Facebook."

"Well, I didn't forget because I love my phone almost as much as I love you. Hey, Coach P is waving at you. Better go before he freaks."

Nodding, Callie pushed through the weird feelings inside her mind and body. She blew air kisses then took the bleacher stairs two at a time.

"CeeCee! Be careful! The last thing you need is to trip and fall!"

"Okay, Mom. Love you."

"Love you. Got the camera focused and ready! Run, CeeCee, run!"

Rolling her eyes at the way her mother said the phrase as though Callie was Forest Gump, she ran back to her coach, concentrating only on his heavy southern drawl while he gave her tips on the upcoming race. Focus zeroed back to where it should be. Callie was ready when the race was announced over the speakers.

"Runners: take your marks."

"For you, my brother," Callie whispered as she settled into her position in lane one. Taking a deep breath, she stared ahead, eyes focused on the small space between the white lines. She could do this; she *would* do this, or the hope of college was out of the question. Tuition for two children was impossible to swing for her parents—but if only for one—it could be done. Having the worry off her shoulders would make senior year all the more memorable.

Shutting out all outside distractions, Callie embraced the adrenaline rush and let it take hold.

Bam!

Bursting forward at the sound of the gun, Callie's long legs ate up the track with loping strides, arms pumping in a controlled, even rhythm. She visualized the finish line and pushed her body to its limit when she sensed another runner gaining ground at the end of the third lap.

Oh, no you don't! This is for me and my brother! Callie thought while gritting her teeth.

Digging from deep reserves, Callie thundered down the lane, ignoring the burn in her thighs and chest. The roar from the stands barely registered as blood pounded inside her ears.

Fifty. Thirty. Fifteen. Ten. Almost there! Razorbacks here I come!

Breaking tradition and Coach Patterson's stern warnings about not looking at the clock, Callie let her gaze flicker to the infield for a brief second. Either she was hallucinating or she was truly about to break her own personal best *and* the state record.

As she crossed the finish line and glanced at her amazing time of 5:01, pride swelled in her chest. She'd done it! Put her mind to it and accomplished the lofty goal. Callie looked up to where her family always sat, hoping her brother and father made it in time to see the amazing achievement—one that would change the family for the better.

The seats were empty.

Callie didn't have a chance to continue searching for Kevin or her family. Coach Patterson and the rest of the team surrounded her, shouting and jumping up and down with excitement.

"You did it! You broke the state record!" Rachel McGovern screamed.

"Way to go, Callie! Damn but that was amazing!" yelled Sheri Talbot. "You hauled ass!"

"Hey, Coach P? Looks like you're getting a raise!" shouted someone else from behind Callie.

"I knew you could do it, CeeCee! I just knew it!" Coach Patterson exclaimed, beaming with pride. "I couldn't be any prouder even if you were my own daughter! You'll have your pick of any college now, but please choose the Hogs, okay?"

Coach Patterson winked and Callie laughed. "Rumors were true, huh Coach?"

"I don't know what you're talking about," Coach Patterson

responded with heavy sarcasm. "Come on all my Raging Wildcats. We've got to get off the track before the next race."

The happy group migrated to the infield, minus Callie. She was determined to find her family and share the amazing time together. Without all their love and support, especially Colton and her father's, she'd have never achieved this moment.

"Callie?"

Scanning the seats, Callie searched for any signs of her family. The heavy sense of dread roared back, so strong this time it was like someone had their arms around her chest, squeezing the air from her lungs. Though still light outside, the entire field darkened from the outer edges inward. The dull throb in her legs and back spiked to burning pain. It took a lot of effort to answer Coach Patterson. "I'll be there in a minute. I want to see if my mom remembered how to use the video camera."

"Don't worry if she didn't. I made sure some of the yearbook staff came to cover the meet. I gave strict instructions to…"

Coach Patterson's voice mixed with the sounds of the crowd and the students. Converging together, they morphed into white background noise the second Callie finally spotted Kevin and her mother near the concession stand.

Three cops surrounded them and one held her mother as she sobbed into his burly chest.

The dread disappeared.

Cold fear took its place.

Callie didn't remember walking yet soon found herself only feet away, the wails of her mother piercing the early evening.

"No. God, not them both! Not them both at the same time! Joe. Colton. No!"

Pain exploded from Callie's legs and back, engulfing her entire body and mind. The bond with Colton—the unexplainable connection only shared by twins—was severed.

Permanently.

Callie felt it burst from her chest. The warmth of the connection disappeared, leaving her soul cut in half and in the dark. "Mommy?" Callie asked in a quiet whisper.

"Oh, baby, I'm so sorry," Kevin said.

The darkness crept closer. Dizziness and confusion set in. Callie felt Kevin's arms around her shoulders yet couldn't remember seeing him walk to her side. Still staring at her mother sobbing in the arms of a stranger, the world felt off balance. Her mother didn't answer. Callie wondered if she'd even heard her speak.

Turning her face to Kevin's, Callie's voice was barely audible. "The wreck on 40—it was them, wasn't it?"

"Yes," Kevin choked out.

The world went dark and swallowed Callie Claire Novak—fraternal twin to Colton Caleb Novak and daughter of Joseph Jeffrey Novak—destroying any semblance of her previous life in one, giant gulp.

"Did you know?"

The question wasn't accusatory, only asked in a breathy, mumbled whisper. Her mother's voice was almost gone, vocal chords inflamed from hours upon hours of crying and several anxiety pills taken since they'd arrived home after the horrible visit to the morgue.

Callie forced her body to remain still, afraid her mother would feel the tension in her muscles. Licking her lips, Callie snuggled closer, burying her face against her mom's shoulder while she lied. "No."

The ploy didn't work. Shrugging away, her mother stood and glared down, her body swaying just a hair from the pills and exhaustion. "Callie Claire…don't you lie to me. Not now. I need—no, I *want*—to know the truth. Did you know Colton was using drugs?"

Though still numb from the news, a flicker of anger sparked inside Callie's chest. The protectiveness over her frailer, less athletic, and creatively-inclined twin still remained. "I said no, and I meant no, Mom."

Another round of tears came, racing down her mother's cheeks. Callie's heart melted at seeing the usually vibrant and happy-go-lucky Annie Novak look so grief stricken. Losing her husband and son at the same time seemed to have aged her twenty years in less than half-a-day. Lack of sleep hadn't helped any either.

"I just—God, I can't believe this happened! I had no clue. Neither did your father. How in the world did we miss the signs?"

"Mom, he's been on anxiety medication for over a year, remember? After that bully beat him up at school? He hasn't been the same since."

"Those were prescribed to him, just like me, Callie! It's not the same!"

Callie held her tongue. Drugs were drugs—prescription or legal—at least in her book. Ever since fourth grade, she feared taking even an aspirin in case she was ever tested before a meet. She'd seen it happen to other athletes and vowed all her hard work wouldn't be wasted. She didn't even take medication for her horrible cramps.

Colton may have started out on Xanax to manage his stress levels, but obviously, it wasn't enough. Callie demanded proof after the deputy informed them Colton told the paramedics it was his fault for driving while high and then mentioned what they found in Colton's backpack at the coroner's office.

Since the pack was locked in the evidence room at the sheriff's department, the deputy clicked around on his phone, producing photos taken from the accident scene. Sure enough, a small case no bigger than one of Callie's manicure kits was inside the backpack, a used needle and dirty spoon resting next to an empty baggie.

Callie played dumb when she saw it even though she recognized the sleek black case. She'd seen it in Colton's room several times and naively assumed it housed drawing tools.

It was at that precise moment, staring at the cold truth, blips of nagging worry about Colton—the brief flashes of concern she'd tossed aside as simple jealousy over her achievements—converged into the ugly truth. In the back of her mind, Callie always knew yet refused to accept.

When it dawned on her Colton had been trapped inside the demolished SUV, still alive just as she started the race, his legs and back crushed, she threw up all over the floor of the morgue waiting room. Truly, she'd felt her brother's pain up until their mystical connection broke.

Though it wouldn't be official until an autopsy was performed, Callie didn't need to wait for the results.

Colton had been high on heroin and killed himself and his father in a five-car accident. The cop said it was a miracle all the others involved suffered only minor injuries. He'd questioned the two of them, asking if either of them were aware Colton was using drugs and why—if they knew or suspected—Mr. Novak allowed him to drive. The conversation sent her mother into a hysterical crying jag, ending when Callie told the cop to stop being such a callous ass and led her sobbing mother to the parking lot.

Pacing around in small, wobbly, circles, her mother continued to ramble. "We never saw any signs other than him being a bit moodier than normal and wearing sunglasses more often. I thought it was hormones and teenage angst, you know? Colton's grades never slipped, he kept up with the same friends, never stopped drawing or painting."

Callie stood and reached for her mother. Instead of a welcoming embrace, she turned away. Momentarily stunned by the rejection, Callie bit her to keep the tears away. "Colton was a fragile soul, Mom. Creative minds usually are—at least that's what I remember reading somewhere. He didn't have an outlet to release his anxiety physically like I do."

"Promise me, Callie—you didn't know? Never suspected? I know how close you two are—were."

Drawing strength from the same place she did when running, Callie didn't even blink or change the tone in her voice. "Promise, Mom. I loved Colton. If I thought something was wrong, I would have told you or Dad."

Walking over to the edge of the couch, her mother bent down and picked up Colton's favorite hat. Pulling it to her chest, the tears came again. Without a word, her mother walked up the stairs to her room, leaving a heartbroken Callie alone to deal with the tragedy.

Grabbing her cell off the end table, Callie winced. She'd missed eight calls, had forty-three unread text messages, and saw countless notifications from Facebook. The only person she even considered calling was Kevin, yet she couldn't get her fingers to touch the keys and dial.

She'd always been high-strung, mind constantly spinning with a myriad of thoughts and worries. There was no way she'd be able to carry on any sort of intelligent, coherent conversation with anyone, so she headed upstairs to Colton's room.

It was time to spy, to search for what she'd obviously missed and to try and reconnect with him.

Callie's breath caught in her throat when she opened the door. The familiar scent of Colton—a wonderful mixture of spicy cologne, his personal musk, and a hint of acrylic paint—made her gasp. How long would it be, even if they sealed his room tight, before the smell of the person she loved the most in the world disappeared?

Closing the door behind her, Callie flicked on the light. She started in his closet, methodically going through every nook, crevice, and hiding spot, finding nothing out of the ordinary.

Annoyed, she walked over to the desk and touched the screen on his laptop. To her surprise, it turned on.

Colton hadn't logged out of Facebook.

Callie spent over an hour reading all Colton's private messages, hoping she'd find one that might give her a clue what was going on inside his mind.

She didn't. Colton had been careful, never revealing to anyone online anything that could be construed as odd or strange. There were no messages or posts about one thing drug related. No cryptic words suggesting even a hint of being high. The only thing odd was Colton hadn't been as active online during the past four months.

Right around the time she'd stepped up her training.

Frustrated, Callie stood and stretched, looking around the room one more time.

She hadn't checked the bed.

Feeling under the mattress, her fingers touched something cold. Clamping her fingers around it, she pulled.

A needle.

"My God, brother. Why?"

In a fit of anger, Callie flipped the mattress, uncovering a drawing pad and journal. She opened the journal up first, scanning the pages. Colton had terrible penmanship for someone who could draw and paint beautiful renditions of anything in front of him.

The Herd

Surrender all you know; let pride and jealousy go.

Only once you fall are you free

To do anything at all.

We all struggle for inner peace, but first we must confront the beast.

That grinding monster that lives within; the dirty evil that makes us sin.

Beaten to a pulp tonight; time to decide if you will stand and fight.

Or will you back down and cower? No, stand up and devour!

No more options; no more time.

Start to lead or fall behind.

Get on your feet, or be led like sheep.

Wiping away the tears streaming down her face, Callie looked at the date. Colton had written the poem only days after Callie had beaten the crap out of Reggie Cartwright, the bully who jumped Colton after school. Though just shy of six feet, Colton wasn't a fighter. He never had been. Callie had always been the mouth *and* the brawn. Some of her friends, including Kevin, had given her a hard time about interfering in her brother's business. When her father found out, he was proud on one hand his daughter was such a tough cookie yet embarrassed and ashamed on the other because his son was weak.

Turning to the back pages, Callie read another poem written only two weeks prior.

The Path of Truth
I can't find my way
Lost in route for so long.
Without happiness today
God, nirvana will never come along.
Overcome by it all I slide,
There is no more fear;
No more pride.
The monster made it all disappear.
Today I quit believing
It lies and gives no favors.
It is all about deceiving
These hits are no saviors.
If I continue
It will destroy me.
It's just a taker
That will never set me free.

Callie stared at the poem, dumbstruck. Colton's words were full of heartbreak and fear. She couldn't believe she never realized how much emotional pain filled her brother's mind. Hands shaking, Callie flipped to the last page, written only three days ago.

White Knight
Your honey-filled words dripped sweetly into my ear; I heard.
Your delicious aroma wafted gently into my nostrils; I smelled.
Your stunning visuals opened my tear-stained eyes; I saw.
Your tender caresses glided easily through my fingers; I felt.
You slid so gracefully inside my sad, pain-filled mind; I became.
I turned into someone else; an empty husk of bones; I'm lost.
Your words seduced me, and I can't tune them out; I scream.
Your scent sickens me, yet I inhale deeply; I drown.
Powder turns to liquid and goes smoothly in; I lose.
I am no more; a monster now resides. You win.

"Oh, Colton," Callie sobbed. "Why didn't you tell me you were in such trouble? God, I'm so sorry I ignored the signs, but you should have come to me!"

Callie opened the drawing pad, surprised to find it only had one picture. A dark blue butterfly was on the ground, its wings tattered and torn. Next to it was a needle, a set of ominous, orange-red eyes stared from a dark sky above. Flecks of paint starting at the top down to the still, delicate creature showed the trajectory of its fall. Colton had titled it "Ruined Wings."

Hugging the journal and pad to her chest, Callie sank to the floor, sobbing at her brother's pain. Sadness and remorse competed for control, heartbroken she'd missed her brother slowly dying while she'd been focused on only achieving her own, selfish pursuits.

The emotional turmoil inside Callie's heart, the pain of losing her best friend and her amazing father, drove her to near hysteria. She wanted to scream…wanted to hit something—unleash the fury at the senselessness of it all.

"No, I want to hurt someone. And as soon as I find out who sold Colton heroin, I will."

2

CHAPTER TWO

Two Weeks Later

"Callie, don't do this. It won't bring them back."

Ignoring Kevin's plea, Callie finished lacing her running shoes then glanced at her watch. It was ten p.m. Kevin's curfew was eleven, so she had to hurry. "You think I don't know that?"

Moving to block her path to the bedroom door, Kevin stood firm. "I won't let you go all vigilante on me like some fictional comic book character. This is real life, and confronting De'Shawn is dangerous, not to mention incredibly stupid. There are other ways—healthier ways—to deal with your pain and grief. This isn't one of them."

"Get out of my way, Kevin," Callie replied, her voice taut with tension. "I know what I'm doing."

"Does your mother? If not, maybe we should go ask her opinion about her seventeen-year-old daughter's plans to find a drug dealer and beat his ass? Maybe also ask her thoughts about you turning down the scholarship to U of A too?" Kevin countered.

The anger that had been Callie's constant companion for over two weeks, urging her to do things her heart knew was wrong, took over. "Kevin? If you breathe one word about those things to anyone, especially my mother, we're done. I mean it. She's barely hanging on as it is after the funeral. Picking out clothes for Colton and Dad to wear, *for eternity,* broke her spirit. She's been so barred out she doesn't even know what day it is. She said Dr. Brunson upped her medication, but I doubt that because she hasn't gone to see him. It's just an excuse she's concocted, relieving her from having to deal with this shit. I'm not leaving her alone and attending college over four hours away! I'll just go to UALR. She needs me."

"I agree—she needs you to be here and safe—which leads me back to my original point."

"I'm doing what she can't, which is dish out a bit of revenge to the bastard who ruined our lives. Move."

"De'Shawn didn't force Colton at gunpoint to use, CeeCee. That was his choice. It was also his choice to get behind the wheel when high. A bit of your dad's fault, too, since he'd had a few beers and let his son drive."

Fury rendered Callie mute. For a few seconds, the two—who'd known each other since fifth grade and had been dating for three years—stared at each other, neither one budging. Kevin was three inches taller than Callie and outweighed her by at least forty pounds.

She didn't care nor did she back down.

"Fine, I know that look and when I've lost an argument. But I'm coming with you," Kevin muttered while moving away from the door. "You'll need some muscle. De'Shawn's got a bad rep and hangs out with some major thugs."

"No. This is my choice, my burden. Not yours," Callie muttered as she stepped into the dark hallway. "I just need you to say I was with you if ever asked by anyone."

"You wouldn't have told me your plans unless secretly you wanted my help," Kevin remarked as they made their way downstairs. "Am I wrong?"

Grimacing, Callie answered, "I hate it when you pick apart my words and actions."

Grabbing her arm, Kevin pulled Callie closer. "You used to love my analytical brain. And I've always loved your spirit, your drive. All the fire, the real grit and determination to get things done others would find too scary. You have this insane ability to focus on a goal and stop at nothing to achieve it. Did you forget what you accomplished two weeks ago on the track? You trained for years then threw it all away! That's not the girl I love. That's the action of a distraught, grief-stricken person not thinking straight."

A pang of regret punched Callie in the gut. Coach Patterson had tried several times to reach out to her, especially when he found out she'd rejected the scholarship, yet she ignored him. The accolades for the win—and the win itself—seemed pointless and trivial now. Colton was dead, and since he'd been the reason she'd pushed herself so hard, why bother? "None of that matters now."

"You're wrong, CeeCee. You, and what you've done, matter. To me. To your mom. All those characteristics are what drew me to you. But this? You've crossed over into someplace else…turned into someone I don't recognize. You're letting your emotions take over, which is why I think you told me. A part of you knew I would be the voice of reason—the logical side—talking you down before you do something you'll regret later."

Pulling away, Callie walked to the front door. "Wrong. I'll regret sitting on my ass and doing nothing for my brother and father later in life. Things can't get any worse, Kevin. They can't. This is what I need to do to move on."

Catching up to her, Kevin whispered, "You've always fought battles that weren't yours to fight. Sometimes things just happen in life, and we have to accept them and move on. Learn not to make the same choices or mistakes. Bad things happen to good people too."

"Don't get all philosophical on me, Kevin. It's easy to preach that crap when it isn't happening to you or your family. De'Shawn Majors lured my brother into a world he never should have been in."

"So what, you're going to stroll up to his place, knock on the door, give him a piece of your mind and he's going to have some epiphany and change his ways? Apologize for destroying your world and attempt to make amends or give up the lifestyle he's chosen? It's nothing but fantasy and fiction Callie—fantasy and fiction. He'll eat you alive and spit out your bones."

"Do you really think I'm that dense, Kevin? I know nothing I say to the sleazebag will hurt him. He's probably burned too many brain cells to realize what he's done anyway."

A weird look crossed Kevin's face. He took a tentative step backward. "Are you…planning on killing him?"

Despite the dire subject matter, Callie laughed. "If I didn't know better, I'd ask if you're high. What, do really think I've turned into a sadistic killer overnight? I'm just going to tell him what a lowlife bastard he is, get him to admit out loud he sold Colton drugs while I secretly record the conversation on my phone, and then take it to the police."

Kevin looked doubtful. "I call bullshit. You plan on confronting him, letting that mouth of yours run wild, provoking him until he attacks you. I know you think you can handle yourself, but you're wrong, CeeCee. Let the police deal with him. That's what they're trained to do."

Callie grabbed the door handle. "This discussion is over. Try and stop me and I'll just wait and do it when you aren't around. I'll be back before eleven. If Mom wakes up, just tell her I went for a run to clear my head."

"CeeCee, wait!"

Ignoring Kevin's plea, Callie burst out the door. He tried to catch her, but Callie was faster. She fled into the night, feet pounding the street as though the devil was right behind her. Kevin's footfalls stopped after the first two blocks.

Callie never looked back, determined to confront De'Shawn Majors.

Stopping at the intersection of 8th and Cross, Callie was breathing hard from running the entire time. A siren wailed in the distance, and several dogs howled in protest. A light breeze fluttered through her damp hair. Callie made her way toward 139 8th Street, moving toward the two-bedroom HUD house where De'Shawn Majors lived.

Four days ago, when Callie confronted Colton's best friend Richard after the funeral, she'd berated him until he cracked. Finally, Richard admitted he knew about Colton's drug use, where he got it from, and how he'd even tried it a few times. Richard sobbed, begging Callie to forgive him. When she wouldn't, he'd gotten angry and said it was her fault Colton sought out drugs.

"Do you have any idea how humiliated Colton was when you beat up Reggie Cartwright? It made him feel like a loser—one who needed his sister to fight his battles. He loved you but hated you at the same time. God, he wanted more than anything to be tough like you, but it wasn't who he was. You beat up a bully, but you never saw how your actions beat him up mentally too."

The words pierced Callie's soul, making her angrier than she'd ever been.

More fuel to the ever-growing fires inside her mind.

The only way she knew how to put out the flames was unleash the rage inside her on De'Shawn.

Only three houses away, Callie slowed down, gaze scanning the unfamiliar area. She remembered De'Shawn from junior high yet hadn't seen him in years after he dropped out. He'd been on the track team too and was an amazing runner until he tested positive for steroids. Rumors around school swirled about De'Shawn joining a gang, getting arrested multiple times, and his mother going to prison for dealing drugs.

The sounds and smells of the dark street made her bravado from earlier disappear. "What the hell am I doing?" Callie whispered. "Kevin's right: this won't bring Dad or Colton back. Maybe I should tell the cops what Richard said and let them handle things? If De'Shawn is truly as bad as his reputation, they already know about him anyway. I won't confront him. I'll just get a video of illegal activity and take it to the police."

Tamping down her fears at the scary sounds and weird smells of the night, Callie fiddled with her phone and turned on the video camera.

"Girl, I ain't seen muscles like that on any of the other ho's around here. I want me some. How much?"

Spinning around, Callie found herself face-to-face with a man at least four inches taller than her 5'11" frame. He smelled odd—a weird combination of alcohol, cigarettes, and a hint of skunk. The freaky grin on his face while licking his lips made Callie's stomach clench.

Finding her voice, Callie shot back, "You're barking up the wrong tree, mister. I'm not a hooker. Just out for a run on a nice evening and got turned around."

Stepping closer, the man's beady eyes took in every inch of Callie's body. "No one comes around here unless looking to score one way or another. You're one of those rich kids from Hillcrest, ain't ya? Snuck outta the house to get some relief from your stressful life?"

Without conscious thought, Callie had been slowly backing up. She didn't realize how many steps she'd taken until another voice behind her said, "I'll be damned; it's another Novak looking to get high."

Glancing to the left, Callie froze when she noticed De'Shawn was only feet away, surrounded by three men who looked like they just stepped out of prison.

Trapped between the group, Callie stiffened.

"Chica ain't never been high; just look at her. She's one of those health nuts from the good side of town," the man on De'Shawn's right said.

De'Shawn laughed. "You're right, Juan. Haven't you heard the news? Ol' long legs here broke the state record in the women's 1600 two weeks ago. You know, the same day her bro and dad became permanent stains on I-40?"

"No wonder she's got such a nice ass. A *runner's* ass," Juan said.

Callie's stomach juices were close to spewing all over the pavement. She forced the wave of nausea away.

De'Shawn was only inches from her face, his breath foul and warm. "I bet I know why you're here, Callie. You planned on making me pay for Colton's death, right? Some snitch told you I was his dealer, huh? Oh, boo-hoo. The big, bad De'Shawn hurt your wimpy-ass brother, just like ol' Reggie did, and the star athlete steps in to make things right. Too bad you didn't pay more attention to the panty-waste while he was still alive."

The intense fear inside Callie's mind switched to anger. Though she knew the situation was tenuous at best, Callie didn't care. It was too late to run, and this was what she wanted to begin with—a confession on video. "I came here to tell you what a piece of shit I think you are, De'Shawn. You're nothing but a washed-up athlete who turned into a worthless drug dealer selling poison to people with no remorse. I wanted you to know how devastated my mother and I are—"

"Damn, she ain't no ho, that's for sure," the man who smelled like skunk mumbled while walking away.

"No, she's just a stupid, stupid girl for coming over to this side of town," De'Shawn said, his voice low, sinister.

Callie realized the men had flanked her, and the only way out was straight past De'Shawn. Gripping her phone, muscles itching to run as adrenaline spread throughout her body, Callie lunged. The quick movements momentarily stunned the others. Lowering her shoulder, she plowed into De'Shawn, nearly knocking him over.

"Leave her alone!"

Callie's heart skipped two beats at the sound of Kevin's voice.

The rest happened so fast, Callie never had a chance to really digest it all. One minute she was running and the next, she was face down on the pavement, the heavy weight of a body on top of hers.

"Get off her!" Kevin screamed.

Then, a shot rang out at the same time a hand grabbed her hair and slammed her face into the hard pavement. Burning pain exploded in Callie's head. Stars appeared as something hot and sticky ran down her face. She tried to scramble away but couldn't move.

"Make sure his body ain't ever found," De'Shawn yelled.

"Sure thing, Mookie," another answered.

"Take her inside, and let's show her what happens to nosy bitches when they try to mess with us. Destroy that phone," De'Shawn hissed.

Oh, God! Kevin! Why did you follow me? was the last thought Callie had before succumbing to the darkness.

Jerking awake with such force she fell off the bed, Callie landed on the floor with a loud *thump.* Scrambling to her feet, brain still fuzzy and vision blurry from tears, she spun in a complete circle, ready to attack and kill anyone near her, especially the bastard who'd shot Kevin.

Heart racing and mind spinning at full throttle, Callie's shoulders sagged with relief as the sights and smells of her room brought her out of the funk. "God, it was just a dream!"

A soft knock on the bedroom door made her jump.

"Honey, you okay?"

Wiping the tears from her face, Callie hid Colton's journal and pad between the mattresses. "Yeah, just a bad dream. Sorry if I woke you up."

Callie stashed Colton's things away just as her mother walked in and joined her on the bed. "I'm glad to hear you were at least getting some rest, though I'm sorry about the bad dream. They're to be expected for a while. I've been suffering from them too. Want to tell me about it?"

"Not really," Callie lied.

The truth was she did want to talk about it. Callie wanted to say a lot of things but worried her mother was still too fragile to hear all of her rambling thoughts. She'd pushed most of her other relationships to the back burner while she'd been in training—except her family and Kevin—leaving her with no close girlfriends to share or talk to. At least not any she really trusted. That never bothered her before—until now.

"If you change your mind, I'm here…ready to listen. If you don't want to talk to me about what you're feeling, perhaps a counselor would be a better choice? After what we've been through, seeing one is a good idea. I could schedule us some visits in a flash. You know, an impartial stranger to vent to without worry of upsetting—"

"No, Mom. I'll be okay," Callie interrupted. The thought of baring her inner thoughts and struggles to someone she didn't know, a person only listening because they were getting paid to, made her feel weird. "I mean you can go, but it's not for me. I just…I wish I could sleep and not be plagued with nightmares. At least for a solid eight hours."

Making clucking noises with her tongue while studying Callie's face, her mother said, "God, I've neglected you while I've been stuck in my own sorrow. I'm sorry, baby. You look like you need a good, home-cooked meal. For that matter, so do I. Hope there's some food left downstairs to cook."

Callie rolled her eyes. "There's plenty, Mom. The track team brought enough the day of the funeral to feed us for a month, remember?"

"Actually, no. There's been too much going on for me to think straight."

Callie reached for her mother's hand and squeezed. "I know, Mom. Stop worrying. I've been drinking my protein shakes and eating light, just like I do while training. I'm fine. No need to coddle me. I'm not a little kid anymore."

"No, you certainly aren't little anymore, but I still say you need food. Real food. I'm feeling better now, so I'm going to cook dinner for us both."

"It's after ten, Mom! It's not healthy to eat this late."

"You aren't training anymore, honey, and basically starving yourself isn't healthy either. No arguments, Callie. Please? Let me do this. Let me take care of my last…"

Her mother stopped in mid-sentence as tears clogged her throat. Callie felt like an ass. "Okay, Mom. Okay. You win. Downstairs are plenty of the biggest, calorie-riddled, artery-clogging southern dishes to reheat. I'll eat some, but only if I temper it with a protein drink. Deal?"

Beaming, her mother stood, clapping like an excited little girl. "Deal! Yum!"

Watching her mother dash from the bedroom with a bit of the former zest for life sparkling across her face made Callie smile. "God, when will this get any easier?" Callie mumbled under her breath. "No, stop that! The road ahead will be painful and tough, but we'll make it."

She waited until the sounds of dishes rattling in the kitchen drifted upstairs before calling Kevin.

"So much for getting some rest," Kevin teased after answering on the third ring. "I hope your insomnia isn't because of our argument earlier."

"No, it's not you. Promise."

"Good. I'm sorry if what I said upset you, but I meant it. Your plan to go visit De'Shawn was a disaster in the making."

A shiver of fear danced up Callie's spine. The dream was part their real-life conversation, up to the point of Kevin leaving after convincing Callie to stop wallowing in a pit of dark revenge. The rest was her mind's interpretation of what *might* have happened had she followed through with her plans. She changed the subject. "If I keep having nightmares, I'll never sleep again."

"Isn't that a line from a movie or something?"

Callie grinned. "Good job you non-horror film fan! Bonus points if you can name the movie."

"Not fair, CeeCee. You know I don't watch those kinds of flicks. I like movies about things that really happen, not fictional blood and gore with superhuman monsters that never seem to die."

"Those are the best kinds! They let your mind take a break from reality."

"How about I sneak over later? I could be a real, live dreamcatcher. We'll make up like couples are supposed to by getting naked."

Hesitating for a second, Callie considered the offer. Their intimate relationship started six months prior, though during the last two months of intense training, Callie had spurned Kevin's numerous advances. After the awful nightmare of him dying, it was tempting. Snuggling up to and falling asleep in Kevin's arms would be wonderful, yet the compulsion to spend some time with her mother won out. "Lovely idea, but I'll pass. Mom's coming around and actually downstairs fixing dinner. I need to spend some time with her now that's not barred out, okay?"

"Cut her some slack, CeeCee. She's been through a lot too. It's only been what…two years since her parents died while at the lake?"

"We *all* experienced grief after Gram and Grampa drowned. Dad started drinking more and Mom became friends with Xanax. It was less than six months later when Colton got beat up, so maybe all of that contributed to his decision to use harder drugs. I don't know. What I do know is I didn't go down that path."

"No, you didn't. Instead, you channeled all your energy into running. It became your—" Kevin paused and cleared his throat. "This will give you two a chance to talk about school."

"Kevin, don't go—"

"Too late, I went there. You haven't told her you turned down Fayetteville yet, have you?"

"No, but it won't be a big deal when I tell her about UALR. I finally had a chance to look through the stack of mail a few hours ago. The offer letter came today."

"You accepted?"

"Yep. I signed the dotted line less than three hours ago. I'll mail it back to them tomorrow."

"That's going to put a major crimp in our ability to see each other. Russellville is a lot closer to Fayetteville. We'll be hours apart if you stay in Little Rock. I still think you should talk to Coach Patterson and see if he can—"

"No," Callie interrupted. "I've already made up my mind. He can just find another star athlete to mentor for his raise. I'm all Mom has left now. You know neither of my parents had any siblings."

"Yes, I know. And your dad was raised in foster care. I remember. Just the two of you—I get that."

"How in the world could I study and concentrate on training if all I did was worry about her, Kevin? Fayetteville is out of the question. Enough of this topic. What are you doing tomorrow?"

"Okay, okay. I'll stop beating that dead horse. We'll figure out a plan to see each other in college. I'll just put a lot of miles on my car. So, what am I doing tomorrow? Well, whatever you are, baby. We've got one week to spend every day together before I start my summer job. I'm glad to be a runner at Glover & Glover, but I feel bad now with what's happened. Maybe I could try and get you hired on as a runner too?"

Callie smiled as a rush of love flowed through her body. Kevin was always looking out for her best interests. "You're so sweet, but I think you've forgotten I'll need a vehicle to run errands. I doubt we can tag-team it."

"Wow, I must be tired. You're right. Well, maybe they have an opening for a receptionist or something. I'll check."

"Thank you."

"Okay, so really, what are we doing tomorrow? Movie? Hiking? Lake day?"

"You get to hold my hand while I get a tattoo."

Kevin burst out laughing. "You? A tattoo? That's hysterical. Seriously, what are we doing?"

Bristling, Callie countered, "I've wanted one for a long time."

"Uh-huh. I've known you for *years*, and you've never once said anything about getting inked. In fact, you always said people with—"

"Yes, I'm aware of what I said out loud. It's a different story inside my private thoughts. I said those things because I never could figure out what design I wanted. Now, I have the perfect one in mind. It's a butterfly Colton painted."

"Your mom's okay with this?" Kevin asked.

"What I do to my body is none of her business," Callie answered, hoping she didn't sound as annoyed as she felt. Though she loved him, Kevin was quite pushy at times. His judgmental tone and sarcasm wasn't helping, either.

"Not according to the law. You have to be eighteen to get a tat or have parental consent."

Callie snorted. "You and you're obsession with following every little rule!"

"That's why I'll make an amazing lawyer," Kevin teased.

"I swear, sometimes you act just like an old man. Not to worry. I've got money, and it speaks louder than ID."

Chuckling, Kevin added, "I forgot I'm chatting with the girl who never takes no for an answer. So, where are you planning this piece of art to be on your body? Fair warning: if you say the lower back, I'm breaking up with you. Don't want my future wife looking like a pole dancer."

"No tramp stamp for me, baby. Top of my foot, thank you very much. Uh-oh, I smell something burning so I guess I should go help Mom."

"How's she holding up?"

"Best as can be expected, I guess. Like me. Seriously, I need to go before she burns the house down. Come over around noon, okay?"

"Can I bring my phone? I've got to video this," Kevin retorted, laughing.

"Fine, but no sharing online."

"You are such a weirdo! All the videos of you running are what caught the attention of scouts, remember?"

"True," Callie muttered, hating when Kevin was right.

"Hey, speaking of online, you should probably post some type of thanks for all the comments. The last I counted, there were 345 posts of sympathy on your profile…even more on Colton's."

"Will you? Do it for me, I mean? You know how much I hate that kind of crap."

"It still baffles me why you have a smartphone yet never use it to its full potential."

"Not true. I use it to text and video chat with you plus the running app. I never got into the whole digital age or the weird obsession to share my personal life with the entire world. This is *not* news to you."

"Another reason you keep me around—my media and tech savviness," Kevin laughed. "You know it. I'll make it nice and sweet. Genuine CeeCee."

"Thank you, babe. I gotta go. Please don't be late tomorrow. I love you."

"Always and forever," Kevin replied.

After disconnecting the call, Callie made her way downstairs, smiling as the smell of burnt food and the sound of humming wafted from the kitchen.

"Mom? Need some help?"

"I think I ruined the broccoli casserole but everything else is almost ready, plus I made you a protein smoothie. Here."

Taking the shake from her mother's hands, Callie gulped down nearly half in one long swig. The amount of food piled onto the table was enough to feed ten people. "Mmm, best one yet, Mom. Thank you."

They sat at the table and talked for nearly forty minutes about safe topics. Things like school, track, scholarships, Kevin, her mother entering the workforce again, and Callie's plans for the summer. They even discussed the pros and cons of getting another dog since Benny, their enormous St. Bernard, died three months prior and no one had seemed ready to get a new puppy. The only subject not mentioned was the incredibly painful losses of the two Novak men.

Though a tad irritated the decision to turn down Fayetteville was made without discussing it first, her mother seemed relieved when Callie told her about UALR and being only twenty minutes away.

A sense of warm peace settled over Callie's chest, spreading to her limbs. Listening to her mother gab, bouncing from one subject to the next, normally drove her crazy.

Tonight was different for some reason. A pleasant fuzziness engulfed her from head to toe. Suddenly, she was exhausted, barely able to keep her eyes open.

"Thanks for the dinner, Mom. It was wonderful. Leave the dishes and I'll get them tomorrow. I'm heading to bed before I pass out in the mashed potatoes."

With a big smile and warm hug, her mother shooed Callie toward the stairs. "No face-planting into food tonight, though it would be funny. A good night's rest is just what the doctor ordered. See you in the morning."

While climbing the stairs, Callie wondered why her legs felt so weird. By the time she reached the door to her room, her vision seemed off. Blinking to clear her head, she worried about how much damage she'd done to her brain from lack of sleep. In the past week, she'd slept maybe a total of ten hours. Callie stumbled toward the bed.

The second her head touched the pillow, overwhelming, unexplainable calmness enveloped her mind. The constant buzzing of thoughts and worries seemed quiet, as though they, too, were ready for a break.

"Everything's gonna be okay. Not normal, but okay," Callie whispered, smiling at the funny way the words came out. "Yep, everything's gonna be okay now."

Bright beams of sunlight burned through her eyelids, warming Callie's exposed skin. Squinting, she shielded her face and rolled over, gasping after noticing the time.

"Eleven thirty! Crap! Why am I still in bed?"

Flinging the sheet off, Callie raced to the bathroom, in a rush to get cleaned up and dressed before Kevin arrived. While showering, it dawned on her she felt revived and fresh, plus she had no memory of any nightmares, only pleasant dreams of her and Colton playing together as children. It was the first time since the awful day on the track she felt somewhat connected to her brother again.

Once finished, Callie dashed into her room, rummaging through the drawers to find some clean shorts and a t-shirt. She heard her mother walking down the hall. "Mom? Have you seen my running shoes?"

"Well, someone looks all bright-eyed and bushy-tailed."

"Why did you let me sleep so late?" Callie mumbled while looking under the bed, "Kevin will be here in less than ten minutes! Ugh! I can't find my shoes!"

"Baby, they're right where you left them—on top of the stairs. My, for someone who got a full night's rest, you sure are antsy. They never affect me that…"

When her mother's words stopped in mid-sentence, Callie poked her head over the mattress and saw her backing out of the room.

"Wait, Mom. What did you mean by that?" Callie asked, though deep inside her heart, she already knew the answer.

"Nothing. I'll go get your shoes."

The heaviness in her limbs, the overwhelming exhaustion the night before, the quiet inside her mind, and a night full of good memories of Colton—it all finally clicked. The knowledge infuriated Callie. "You gave me something last night, didn't you?"

Squaring her shoulders, her mother stepped back inside. "Yes, I crushed up a Xanax and mixed it with your shake. You needed some rest, baby! I knew it would knock you out and let you sleep without having another nightmare, and I was right. You slept a solid twelve hours—"

"I...do you have any idea...if I'm ever tested, my reputation will be trashed!" Callie was so angry she couldn't think straight, words jumbling together as she tried to process the betrayal. "My God, Mother! What the Hell? Dad...Colton...they died because of drugs! You didn't think it was wrong to slip me some?"

"Callie Claire! They're prescription anxiety medication! Stop acting like I gave you morphine!"

"Drugs are drugs, Mom. God, I can't believe you did this to me! I'm outta here!"

Grabbing her purse and phone from the bed, Callie stormed past her mother into the hallway. In one quick swoop, she picked up her shoes then ran down the stairs.

"CeeCee, stop! Come back here and talk to me. It was for your own good, I swear. You needed—"

"You have no idea what I need, Mother. You never have," Callie interrupted while jerking the front door open. "Don't wait up."

Slamming the door behind her, Callie ran to the edge of the driveway, relieved to see Kevin's car pull up to the curb.

"Babe, what's wrong?" Kevin asked.

"Drive. Right now," Callie ordered after jumping into the passenger seat. "Red Dragon Tattoo on Seventh Street."

Nodding once, Kevin drove toward downtown Little Rock without saying a word. Yanking her damp hair into a messy bun, Callie bent down and slipped her shoes on, mumbling under her breath the entire time. It took three attempts to tie the laces since her hands were shaking.

"Your mom didn't approve of the tattoo idea, did she?" Kevin asked.

Callie glared at him. "Let me cool off or you'll see a side of me you won't like."

The tone in her voice worked: Kevin never said another word, not even when they pulled into the parking lot of Red Dragon.

Fuming the entire time, Callie's heart beat erratically. She couldn't believe her mother had done such a foolish thing. Callie wasn't sure what bothered her the most—how her mother deceived her or how much Callie enjoyed the tranquil effect the Xanax had on her frazzled mind.

Once inside, Callie showed the man behind the counter Colton's drawing. After slipping him an additional seventy-five dollars above the price of the tattoo when he balked at her ID, she settled into the chair.

"Aren't you nervous?" Kevin whispered as the stencil was placed on her right foot.

"No."

"You're a brave woman. I'm sweating buckets, and it's not even my skin about to be pricked with a needle."

"Ready?"

Callie nodded once to the scruffy man seated in front of her, both of his arms and neck covered in vibrant ink.

"This is going to sting, so please don't jerk. The pattern is delicate. Whoever created it was quite the artist."

"Yes he was, and I won't," Callie answered.

The man was right: it felt like a horde of bees landed on her foot, yet Callie never flinched.

She welcomed the pain because it shut out the anger, guilt, sadness and grief.

Climbing out onto the roof with Colton's journal clenched in her hand, Callie settled near his favorite spot where he used to paint. The air was heavy and wet with humidity; the cicadas and other night insects seemed especially loud.

The blues, yellows, and reds of the tattoo shimmered under the rays of the moon. Her mother flipped earlier, telling Callie she'd defiled her body, scolding her for doing something permanent on the spur of the moment. The conversation went downhill fast and included yet another shouting match about the Xanax incident. Callie had stormed to her room and slammed the door while her mother cried downstairs.

Staring up at the vibrant moon, Callie let the tears come. She cried for what had been, what would never be, and how the relationship with her mother had soured so fast. Tears raced down her cheeks, dripping onto the rooftop in a steady stream.

Everything inside her was jumbled mess. The pain in her heart physically hurt. She'd never get a hug or high-five from her father again. He wouldn't be there at graduation, the first day of college, another meet. There would be no walk down the aisle on his arm, nor would he experience the joy of becoming a grandparent. She'd always been a daddy's girl.

And Colton. Dear, sweet, sensitive Colton—the boy with a football player's body and the soul of an artist. Quiet, shy, and content with having only a few strong relationships besides his immediate family, Colton's life revolved around art, just as Callie's centered on sports. He'd always been a momma's boy. Dad used to tease them when little, saying their chromosomes got mixed up in the womb.

Colton—the brother she'd been protecting ever since she'd been old enough to recognize he needed someone to stand up for him. He wasn't wired to do it on his own.

Now, he was gone, and so was her father.

Forever.

The finality of it all crushed her spirit.

Wracked with sorrow, Callie curled into a ball and wept, chest heaving with great sobs. "Can't...handle...can't...deal. Daddy. Colton. Why?"

Then, the voice she missed more than anything whispered into her ear, "Take, become, and experience, sister. We'll visit for hours. Promise."

"Colton," Callie choked out while looking around, desperate to see his face yet knowing the voice was only inside her head. "I miss you so much."

"Then let me in. You'll find me by opening your mind."

"What do you mean? How?"

"You're smart enough to figure that out, Sis."

It didn't take long for Callie to realize what Colton meant. "I—no, no way. I can't do that! You know that's not me—not my thing. Didn't you hear me ream Mom out for slipping me a Xanax last night?"

"I did. But don't you recall how much fun we had reliving our childhood?"

Smiling, Callie answered, "I do."

"Then stop being such a worrywart! They're just prescription anxiety medication, not street drugs."

"They aren't prescribed to me, Colton!"

"Still afraid to step out of your comfort zone I see."

Just like their arguments before, Colton was dancing on Callie's last nerve. "You did, and look what happened?"

"Touché," Colton replied.

Silence ensued for the next several minutes. The warm, thin tendril reconnecting her to Colton turned cold. The loss broke through her reservations. "What if I get tested at school? All my hard work would be over in a flash."

"Then I guess this truly is goodbye. You haven't felt enough pain yet to need a way to mask it and let me in."

A sob of anguish burst from Callie's throat. "No, don't go! I *am* hurting, Colton. My heart's ripped out. Our connection is gone! I hear you, but I can't *feel* you. I don't know what to do—how to deal with the grief of you both being gone! Mom wants us to go to counseling, but that won't work because it won't bring either of you back! I want you both here. I need to wake up from this awful nightmare!"

"Being awake is the nightmare, Sis. I'll be waiting. Hurry, Callie. It's really lonely here."

"Where are you, Colton? Heaven? Hell? In-between?"

A low, ominous chuckle filled Callie's mind. "Honestly, I'm not quite sure. All I know is its very, very dark. There's no one around. I need your light to help me find my way again."

Wiping the tears from her cheeks, Callie glanced back at the bedroom window. Without really thinking of what she was doing, or how she'd turned into the world's biggest hypocrite in less than twenty-four hours, she stood and went back inside. Her bare feet were silent while padding down the hallway to her mother's room.

Peeking inside, Callie smiled. As usual, she was in a deep, comatose-like slumber.

The pill bottle was on the nightstand; lid on the floor.

Creeping like a cat stalking its prey, Callie crossed the floor. Reaching out, she snagged a handful of pills.

"White Knights, Sis," Colton's voice whispered inside her head. "I knew you were smart enough to figure this out."

In a flash, Callie was back on the rooftop. She swallowed two pills then leaned back until all the way flat. Staring at the cloudless sky,

Callie waited for the drugs to open a gateway so she could see Colton's face instead of just hearing his voice.

"About time you joined me. I've missed you."

"God, I've missed you," Callie answered, smiling as the multidimensional image of her brother's beautiful face filled her mind. "I'm sorry I wasn't here for you when you needed me the most. Forgive me?"

"Nothing to forgive. You had your life, and I had mine. We simply grew apart. You're here now and that's what matters."

"I did all of it for you. Getting up early…running through the pain. Every bit of sweat and blood was all for you. I feel kind of lost now, unsure what to do next," Callie whispered.

"Let's not talk about the past, Sis. Embrace the now. Look at the beauty all around you; let it flow over your heart and embed itself inside your soul."

"Your creative side hasn't changed any since you've been gone," Callie remarked.

"Change is only possible when breathing, CeeCee. It's too late for me now."

"But not for me," Callie answered, the response directed at herself rather than Colton.

3

CHAPTER THREE

Eight Months Later

"Novak! What in the world is wrong with you? You got rocks in those shoes or something?"

"It's hot, Coach P!" Callie whined between gulps of air.

"That's never bothered you before, Novak. Take those sunglasses off. You probably can't see! Did you forget to stretch? Eat? I swear, it's like you haven't run since the meet last year. Your time is pathetic!"

Her coach was right. During the summer and fall, Callie had scaled way back on her daily runs. She didn't feel the need to rise at four a.m. to train or run again at night. She tried a few times, yet the drive to succeed and the urge to change Colton's life disappeared. The lack of desire wasn't just from losing brother and father either. The Xanax bars she took every night made her more relaxed and less driven. Her grades had slipped too, and during the day, she was edgier and had zero patience with anyone.

Tongue loosened from the after-effects of too many bars the night before, Callie snapped. "Get off my back! Do you have any idea how hard it is for me to step foot onto this track? The memories are painful! Last time I was here, my life turned upside down!"

Coach Patterson's face filled with blood as he stomped across the lane, stopping inches from Callie's face. "What did you just say to me?"

Squaring her shoulders, Callie glared defiantly through the dark lenses at the man she once considered a secondary father-figure. "You heard me."

Pointing toward the gym door, Coach Patterson yelled, "Get off my field, Novak. Hit the showers and come back tomorrow with a better attitude."

"You're still pissed at me for going to UALR, aren't you? Grow up, Coach. Better yet, find someone else to scream at and push to get your big bonus. I don't need this shit."

Anger and a blip of pain flashed behind his eyes. Callie never blinked, even when Coach P's stubby finger grazed the tip of her nose, nearly knocking off the glasses.

"One more word and you're off the team, state record holder or not."

The entire track team watched the spectacle of coach and student as they stood toe-to-toe. Callie felt them staring…heard the whispers and giggles. Anger and embarrassment took over, so she turned and sprinted toward the fieldhouse before another smart remark ended her career.

"Guess she ain't the star anymore," a teammate muttered as Callie ran past him.

Though still running, Callie turned, peddling backward while she gave him the finger.

"Callie, look out!" Coach Patterson yelled.

She tried to turn around in time, but her muscle coordination wasn't in full swing. Callie's legs tangled up with a hurdle, sending her body end over end.

A loud *pop* followed by burning pain in her right knee made her scream after landing on the track.

"Callie!" Coach Patterson ran to her side. "Don't move. I think you dislocated the kneecap. Russell? Go get the stretcher."

Tears of pain streamed down Callie's face as the entire track team formed a tight circle, everyone murmuring words of encouragement. Someone put a cold towel on her head, and others pressed towels on her elbow, thigh and shoulder to stop the bleeding.

"I'm sorry, CeeCee. I let my temper get the best of me. I'm not used to you having an attitude, and honestly, I didn't even think about how being out here would be difficult for you. Don't you worry—I don't think you've done any permanent damage. We'll get you to the hospital to make sure. I'll call your mother and have her meet us there. Okay?"

"No, she's at work. Get Kevin, please? He's in the library, studying. I need Kevin," Callie answered.

"I'll go get him," Rachel McGovern offered.

"Tell him to meet us at Southwest Hospital," Coach Patterson instructed.

A flurry of activity and noise followed after Russell returned. Callie yelped in pain as her body was lifted onto the stretcher. In minutes, she was spread out across the backseat of Coach Patterson's SUV, flying down the highway to the hospital.

Though in pain and fearful her running career was over, Callie worried the hospital might draw blood and test it. Did they do that for a simple dislocation?

God, I hope not. If they do, they'll discover I've been taking Xanax and then my scholarship will be toast. No, I won't let them, even if they want to. It's my body and they can't make me.

"You're a lucky lady, Callie. Very lucky."

Callie glanced up at Doctor Brunson who stood next to the bed, his back to her as he stared at the X-rays of her leg. The shot he'd given her to ease the pain and calm her nerves while resetting her knee made her feel relaxed, wonderful, loopy, and slightly dizzy. "How so?"

"You didn't fracture any bones, so surgery isn't necessary. You only dislocated your kneecap, not your knee, which means no damage to the peroneal nerve. Recuperating from a dislocated knee takes longer and carries greater risks for future re-injury, especially in athletes. If the peroneal nerve is damaged, some patients suffer from foot drop."

"Foot drop? What's that?" Callie muttered while staring at the tattoo on her foot.

"It's when you cannot lift your foot while doing even normal activities like walking or climbing stairs. The condition causes the toes to drag the ground, which makes running nearly impossible."

Smiling, relieved the injury wasn't a career-ending one, Callie asked, "So, when can I take the brace off and start training again?"

When Dr. Brunson turned to face her, Callie's mouth went dry. She could tell from the concerned look he was about to drop news she didn't want to hear. "It's a removable splint, not a brace, and you'll need to wear it for the next three weeks, perhaps longer depending upon how quickly you heal. Also, I'm ordering six visits with a physiotherapist to help you restore movement and function."

Callie's mouth dropped open. "Three weeks? I can't miss that much time training! This is my senior year."

Dr. Brunson's somber, dark brown eyes stared down with a hint of compassion. "Your Coach informed me of your accomplishments and scholarship to UALR. Here's my advice, for what it's worth: sit out your senior year and fully recover before college."

Callie didn't have a chance to respond to the shocking news because her mother burst into the room, looking frazzled and haggard. "Oh, my God! Callie, what happened?"

"I'm okay, Mom. I just tripped over a hurdle on the track and messed up my knee. Dr. Brunson said it's nothing."

Dr. Brunson gave Callie a stern look before turning his attention to her mother. "Good to see you again, Mrs. Novak, though I'm sorry it's under these circumstances. Callie's diagnosis of the injury differs from mine. Though not a major injury, it does require the leg to remain immobile for several weeks and physical therapy to assist in the healing process."

"Thank you for the truth, Dr. Brunson. Callie has a tendency to whitewash bad news, especially when it comes to running."

"Mom, please," Callie interrupted while rolling her eyes. "I'm fine."

Stepping between daughter and mother, Dr. Brunson continued. "I was just telling Callie she can't resume training until fully healed. I'm afraid she didn't take the news too well. Understandable since this is her senior year. However, if she pushes herself too hard or too quickly, I'm afraid permanent damage may be the end result."

"Don't worry, Dr. Brunson. I'll make sure she sticks to whatever treatment plan you set out."

"Good to hear. Now, let me finish up some paperwork and write her prescriptions out so you both can get home. She's to keep the leg elevated as much as possible and no weight on it whatsoever. Call my office and make a follow-up appointment around four weeks from today."

"Pills? What kind of pills?" Callie asked. What if Dr. Brunson wanted her to take something and it didn't mesh well with the Xanax she'd been pilfering for months from her mother's stash? Well, she *had* been, until her mother went back to work and stopped refilling them. Callie had been forced to find other avenues to get the pills.

"Steroids to help with inflammation and some hydrocodone to take for pain only as needed."

Dr. Brunson stepped out of the room, leaving a dazed and confused Callie alone with her distraught mother. Closing her eyes, Callie let the pleasant feeling coursing through her mind and body override the worried murmurs of her mother as she groused about insurance, too many bills, and how in the world she'd pay for them.

"Want some more water or anything to eat?"

Callie smiled at Kevin, enjoying the way he'd fawned and hovered over her like a mother hen for the last four hours. "No, I'm fine."

Kevin rose from the chair, crossing the room to shut the bedroom door. "Now that you're coherent again and your mom's downstairs, I think we need to talk."

She didn't like the tone in his voice. Kevin sounded peeved. "About what?"

"You. Us. How you've changed during the last several months."

A ripple of anger rose inside her chest. Callie did her best to keep it under wraps. "Of course I've changed! My brother and father died on the same day! Am I supposed to just pretend that didn't happen?"

"No."

"Then exactly what are you getting at, Kevin?"

Lowering his voice as he approached the edge of the bed, Kevin replied, "Rumors around school are flying. The word is you've been seen in the bathroom taking pills and even buying some from that lowlife druggie, Lisa Bowers. Several people have told me you've fallen asleep in English and that you're failing math—"

"Math's always been my weakest subject, Kevin. You know that," Callie interrupted.

"Then it's time to get you a tutor. You really don't want to fail, do you?"

"Of course not, but a tutor's impossible. Mom doesn't have the money to pay for one."

"No need. I'll find some math whiz at school to help you out. I'm thinking Ricky Weaver. He's in my Western Civ class, and I'm pretty sure he'd cut off an appendage to spend time with you."

"Nice, Kevin."

"I'm serious. He asks about you a lot, dropping comments here and there about how lucky I am to be dating such an amazing athlete. I'll ask him tomorrow."

"Thank you. Now, are we done with this stupid conversation?"

"Not even close. Rachel mentioned on our way to the hospital about what happened between you and Coach P. She said you were really aggressive, mouthy, *and* you tripped because you weren't paying attention. You were too busy flipping off Tim Landers."

"The last part is true. He said something ugly to me when I ran past him! The rest is a bunch of crap. You know high school is nothing but a place for people to make up stories about others to fill the void in their own lives. It's all bullshit." Callie lied, wondering who in the hell ratted her bathroom activities out. She'd certainly need to be more careful going forward.

The concerned look on Kevin's face changed over to irritation. "You're lying, Callie. Something is going on, and whatever it is isn't just leftover grief from what happened to your dad and Colton. You've been really short-tempered with everyone, including me. Do you realize, or even care, that we haven't made love in months?"

"Uh, you work after school every day and on the weekends, remember? Exactly when are we supposed to get freaky? Midnight on Sundays?"

"That never bothered you before, CeeCee. How many times have I climbed up to the roof and snuck in here? Too many to count—but that's been ages ago. Every time I've brought it up recently, you tell me no. You're too tired. You're sleeping more than usual, and I bet," Kevin reached across the bed for her phone. Callie tried to stop him but wasn't fast enough. "If I check the running app, it will confirm my suspicions."

"Put it down, Kevin!" Callie yelled. "You have no right to—"

"Yep, I'm right. You haven't logged in any hours. Have you hit the pavement at all since the last meet?"

The lie rolled off her tongue with ease. "Of course I have. There's nothing on the app because I screwed it up and had to delete it and start again."

Kevin tossed the phone onto the bed. "Bullshit. You don't do technology, remember? The correct terms are uninstall and reinstall, and you don't know how. I think you're suffering from depression. I talked to your mom while you were sleeping and she said you won't go to counseling with—"

Callie lost it. "You did what?"

"See? That right there—the instant attitude and defensiveness. That's what I'm talking about."

Scooting toward the edge of the bed, mindful of her knee, Callie pointed a finger in Kevin's face. "I don't need to be analyzed or scolded, Kevin. Think long and hard about why today was so difficult for me before you assume I'm on drugs or in need of a straightjacket."

"I'm aware it was your first time back on the track. That's why I was shocked when you asked me to wait in the library for you. I assumed you'd want some moral support. I'm also aware tomorrow is your eighteenth birthday."

"And Colton's" Callie added after swallowing the lump of tears in her throat. The truth was she didn't want Kevin to see her run since she knew her physical state had deteriorated over the months since Colton and her dad died. "You have no idea what's going on inside my head or how much I've suffered. Mom's working now and exhausted when she gets home. You've been busy with work, studying, and school activities. I'm all alone now most of the time. When Mom is here, all she does is worry and stress over money. Thank God she stopped all the sobbing at night. The lawsuits from the accident are freaking her out! She's even talked about filing bankruptcy and moving into a smaller place. I don't want to move, Kevin. This is where I grew up. It's my safe zone."

"And your last connection to them both. I get that," Kevin said, his voice softer and with less edginess. "But you've got to learn to move on with your life, CeeCee. Reconnect with your old friends—you know, the ones you've shunned during the last two years? Because guess what? In less than six months, you'll be in college, living in a dorm with a stranger, doing your own thing. Then again, if you don't pull yourself out of this funk and get your grades up, you won't be going to college."

"It's an athletic scholarship, not academic like yours."

"True, but the prerequisite is that you graduate from high school first."

Throwing her hands up in disgust, Callie said, "What do you want me to say, Kevin? That I'm depressed? Lonely? Sad? Scared? Still full of grief? Worried about freaking everything, including us when college starts and you are hours away in Russellville? I'll be stuck with no way to come visit you since a vehicle is out of the financial cards for me. Okay, there you go—I said it. Yes, I'm a wreck and each day I wake up, I keep hoping I'll feel better, but I don't. It just gets worse. I know I've been moody, but it's not because of drugs. It's because I can't cope with all these changes. They came too fast and too close together. I'm having a hard time grappling with them all."

"Which is why you need to go with your mom to counseling! Let out those feelings to an impartial ear—a person who can provide you tools to cope with the losses. If venting along with your mom is too weird, then simply ask for individual therapy."

Sensing an opening to end the discussion, Callie calmed down. "You're right. I'll start going with Mom."

Eyeing her with a mix of suspicion and hope, Kevin asked, "Smart choice and one that will help you deal in healthy ways with the changes in your life. Just one more question: you promise you aren't using? I mean, I'd sort of understand after all you've been through, but numbing the pain isn't dealing with it, CeeCee. It's just a fake mask. Don't get mad at me for saying this, but what happened to Colton proves my point."

Reaching out for his hand, Callie tamped down the fury at the mention of Colton's name and lied. "I swear, not even aspirin. I mean, the doctor at the emergency room gave me a shot of something, but other than that, no. Just...give me time to work through all this with a counselor, okay? It's not you, I promise. The rumors aren't true. I've never said a peep to or been around Lisa Bowers."

"Callie? Another bouquet of flowers arrived. Mmmm, they are lovely roses and carnations and smell heavenly!"

"Thanks, Mom. I'll send Kevin down to get them and bring them up here. He was just leaving anyway."

Kevin smiled after giving Callie a hug. "I'm glad we had this talk. I've been worried about you. So has your mom. Counseling is the right step. I just know it. I love you, baby. Remember, I'm here for you. Always and forever."

"Me too, babe. Now scoot so I can get some rest. My knee is throbbing."

Kevin exited the room and clomped down the stairs. Callie waited for a few seconds and then reached under the pillow, grabbing the plastic bottle full of Vicodin. She downed three and had just enough time to hide them before Kevin walked back in. "The card says these are from Russell Clayburn. I think the boy's got a crush on you."

"Doesn't matter if he does, baby. You're the only man in my life. Set them over by my computer, okay?"

After arranging the flowers, Kevin grinned then winked. "If you want to video chat later, I'll show you mine if you reciprocate. After midnight, of course, when you're officially eighteen. You know how much I'm a stickler for the rules."

Laughing, Callie shook her head. "Uh, you'll have better luck with that by calling 1-800-Dial-A-Ho. You're too much. Go before you're out after curfew and get into trouble."

"Bummer! I swear I'm going to drag you into the digital age one way or another. Now that you're disabled, I stand a good shot."

"Will you please go?" Callie said while tears from laughing ran down her cheeks. "It hurts to laugh."

"Okay. I'll be here about fifteen minutes earlier than usual. I figure we'll need the extra time to get you downstairs and in the car."

With that, Kevin left. Her mother stopped in minutes later for a final check before going to bed. Callie assured her she was fine and to get some rest. Within fifteen minutes after her mother left, the pills kicked in, easing the pain in her knee, shoulder, and arm. Glancing at the stitches near her elbow, she smiled. She felt nothing, which was nice.

"The best part is the way it quiets the mind, isn't it?"

Closing her eyes at the sound of Colton's voice, Callie smiled when his full, real, perfect face appeared. This time, he wasn't a fuzzy image. It was like he was still alive, full of vibrant color and life. "Yes, it is. This stuff is way better than the Xanax! My God, I had no idea what I was missing. I feel, I don't know, like I'm floating in warm water surrounded by love. And you're really here, inside my mind, not just a hallucination."

"That's because our connection is stronger. Those little bars are only benzos. They're like sparklers—pop, fizzle, and over in a flash. Vicodin is an opiate and allows the mind to expand, and the experience last longer. You've ascended to a higher plane. Isn't it amazing?"

"Oh, yeah. Amazing," Callie whispered, unsure if she said the words out loud or only in her mind.

"You keep taking them that fast and soon, you'll be out. What then?"

"I'll find a way to get more somehow. I'm not giving up this euphoria and the true, real ability to feel close to you again."

"That's my sis—determined to do whatever it takes to get what she wants. Oh, and bravo on standing up for yourself today with that obnoxious coach of yours. He's an asshole. It was about time you told him to fuck off. And your little acting job with Kevin was quite impressive. You pulled off those lies like a pro. I'm proud of you."

"You sound funny, Colton—"

Callie's thoughts and words trailed off as the drugs pulled her into a deep, restful sleep.

4

CHAPTER FOUR

Five Weeks Later

"You've healed up quite nicely, Callie. I'm thrilled you took my advice and adhered to the treatment plan. Everything looks great. No nerve or ligament damage. There's hope for breaking the collegiate record for you still!"

Callie winced while rubbing her knee with sweaty palms. She was jittery, had a pounding headache, and felt sick to her stomach. The original prescription of Vicodin allowed for two refills, but Callie took the last pills five days prior. She missed the effects.

No, she didn't miss them. She *needed* them. Without the pills she'd lost touch with Colton, and it was tearing her up inside.

Doing her best to keep her voice calm, Callie asked, "Then why does it still hurt, Dr. Brunson? Sometimes at night it throbs so bad I can't sleep."

Dr. Brunson pulled a chair out from underneath the desk. Once seated, he studied her face, and the intense scrutiny sent a shiver of fear up Callie's spine.

"Since you're eighteen now, I can't discuss my concerns about you with your mother because of HIPPA laws—at least not without your permission."

"What is there to discuss with Mom?" Callie asked, doing her best to keep her voice neutral. "You just said there's no permanent damage."

Lacing his fingers together, Dr. Brunson leaned forward. "My concerns have nothing to do with your injury, Callie. It's about the pills."

Stunned, Callie blurted out, "What's that supposed to mean? You gave them to me, and I took them. End of story. I can't help the fact my knee still hurts!"

"Vicodin is a temporary fix for physical pain, not emotional pain. Your knee healed—the X-rays and the notes from your physiotherapist give no indication any residual pain should be present. You refilled the prescription—twice—and my concern is that you might have a problem. Some people do yet don't know they are susceptible to addiction until their first taste of chemicals."

"That's ridiculous, Dr. Brunson! I'm not addicted to them! I'm just in pain!"

"I disagree. You're exhibiting several signs of withdrawal. You're sweaty and short-tempered, not to mention lying. I see the need behind your eyes. The craving. I also know what happened to your brother, how your father enjoyed drinking a bit too much, and how much Xanax your mother takes."

"None of that is your business and has nothing to do with me! Isn't it illegal to pry into a patient's life?"

"Callie, have you forgotten I've been your family's primary care physician for years? I only work at the hospital on occasion because I enjoy the rush of the ER. I am fully aware of the issues within your family."

Cringing on the inside, Callie tried to keep her cool. "Again, those things have nothing to do with my knee hurting."

"I disagree. The majority of the medical community agrees addiction is a hereditary trait and like other diseases, can remain dormant until something triggers it to—"

Furious, Callie stood, grabbing her purse from the table. "Think what you like, Dr. Brunson. I'm not a drug addict. Make sure to send the release letter to my coach so I can get back on the track again."

"Callie, wait. I'd like to continue—"

Yanking the door open, Callie stopped and whispered, "One more thing, Dr. Brunson. You don't have my permission to discuss whatever imaginary concerns you have about me with my mother or anyone else for that matter. Period. And since I'm eighteen, I think it's time for me to find a new doctor."

Callie left the examination room in a huff. Kevin stood from his spot in the waiting area, immediately sensing something was wrong. "Bad news?"

Walking past him, Callie headed out the front door into the

parking lot. "Yeah, my doctor's a pompous asshole. Take me home please."

Neither said a word until once inside Kevin's car. After starting the engine, he leaned over and grabbed Callie's hand. "Okay, talk. Are you going to need surgery or something?"

Sighing, Callie answered, "No. He just…I don't know. He was rude and didn't believe me when I told him my knee still hurts. He had the nerve to say it was all in my head."

"Maybe that's something you should explore with your therapist?"

Fuming, Callie bit her tongue to control the anger. Yeah, like she'd say anything of meaning or value to Mikki Taylor, the therapist who watched and listened each week with what Callie considered detached boredom. It took several seconds for her to calm down enough to answer. "Yeah, maybe."

Silence filled the car the rest of the ride home. Callie swiped a kiss on Kevin's cheek then watched him drive away. She waited until his car disappeared from sight before pulling out her phone.

It was four o'clock, and her mom wouldn't be home until after six. If she pushed herself, she'd have just enough time. Callie scrolled through the numbers until she found the one she'd labelled *Renee* and then dialed.

"What's up?"

Smiling, grateful Lisa Bowers answered instead of letting the call go to voicemail, Callie said, "Just got back from a visit with the doctor. The good news is my knee is fine—"

"And the bad news is your knee is fine. Gotcha. Up for your regular?"

"No. Step it up a notch."

"That's gonna be double the price and will take me a few days. You ain't the only one out there hurting."

"Days? I…no, I'll figure something out. Thanks."

"Give me a few minutes, will you? Yikes, you're antsy. I'll text you."

Disconnecting the call, Callie glanced at the front door. She only had twenty dollars in her wallet, which was what she usually paid Lisa for two Xanax bars. Callie ran inside the house and up to her mother's room, knowing she kept cash hidden in an old shoebox on the top shelf of the closet for emergencies.

"She won't miss sixty bucks. Besides, I'll land a job soon since track season is over for me and replace it."

Callie waited for ten minutes, willing a text from Lisa to appear on the screen while pacing in small circles. When it didn't, she stuffed the money into her running pack and then grabbed the house keys and cell phone. Pausing at the door, she decided to leave the cell in case her movements could be traced through GPS. An obscure memory of either Kevin mentioning something along those lines, or maybe even something she'd seen on TV or read online, warned her to leave her steps as clean as possible. Callie shoved the cell into her school bag then sprinted out the door.

While running down the tree-lined sidewalk toward a place she'd only visited in nightmares, a small piece of her mind whispered what she was doing was wrong. It whined and nagged about how far she'd fallen.

Callie ran faster, pushing the thoughts away, driven by urges she didn't understand yet couldn't ignore. Once she arrived at her destination, the fear she'd experienced during the dream was gone, replaced by determination and the overwhelming desire to do whatever necessary to see Colton's face.

Stopping at the edge of the sidewalk, Callie noticed the former athlete on the top porch step, watching her with dark, hooded eyes. His lips curved into a snide grin. A big dog was chained up on the other side of the fence, so Callie didn't open the gate. She kept her face a sea of calm while nodding at De'Shawn.

"Always knew you'd come around. Using's a family affair. Gotta say, it took you longer than I figured after your injury. You all washed up now?"

"How did you—?"

"Word travels fast in this town, especially when it's about a semi-famous athlete. So, blew your knee out?"

"No, I'm fine. Minor injury but to be safe, I'm sitting out the rest of the season."

"Smart girl. Wouldn't want to ruin those legs before college, huh? So, let me guess: you're here for the same thing as your bro?"

Shaking her head, Callie answered, "I'm not a junkie, De'Shawn. I'm still in pain and need some Hydros. My doctor won't refill my prescription, and I'm having trouble finding some. Got any?"

De'Shawn stood and walked over to the gate. The way his gaze moved over Callie's body made her want to punch him in the throat.

"I don't do any deals unless I'm sure they're legit. I'll need to check you for a wire. Come inside. Just watch your step. Ol' Hercules bites."

Once inside the filthy house, Callie ignored the bile rising in her throat as De'Shawn's hands poked and touched every inch of her body.

He removed the running pack, yanking out the keys and cash, tossing the contents onto the couch. Satisfied she wasn't wired, De'Shawn asked, "How many you want?"

The experience was entirely different than dealing with Lisa in the bathroom or the park. Callie swallowed hard, thinking back to all the movies she watched, searching for similar scenes so she'd say the right thing. "I need four."

De'Shawn laughed as he reached around Callie, scooping up the money. "You think eighty bucks is gonna get you four Vicos? That's funny."

Panic welled up in Callie's chest. "Please, I need four. It's what it takes to—"

"To numb the pain inside your head? Yeah, I've heard that before," De'Shawn whispered, inches from Callie's lips. "But you ain't got enough cash, baby."

Callie's voice cracked. "It's all I've got right now! I don't have a job. I can get more tomorrow."

"Cash-n-carry, that's the way this game works. This here eighty dollars only buys two, unless you can think of something else you have to offer as payment? You mentioned you don't have a job?"

Instead of answering, fearful of what was coming next from De'Shawn's mouth, Callie shook her head.

De'Shawn's hands were suddenly on her again, stroking and caressing her back, butt, and crotch. "You've grown up since the last time I saw you on the track and filled out real nice—lots of muscle and curves. So, I'll tell you what, Callie. I'll give you an entire month's supply—for free—in exchange for two things."

Dread filled Callie's heart as she asked, "What things, De'Shawn?"

A sinister grin crossed De'Shawn's face. "Watching you suck my dick then working for me. I need a new dealer at your school. Do me right, sell what I give you each month, and I'll let you have all you want for free—both pills and a big dick."

Though sickened by the proposition, the offer of unlimited pills freed Callie up from the worry of ways to acquire more.

"It's a good deal, sis. Don't let your silly pride or prudishness get in the way! It's just a dick. A few licks and it'll be over. Easy stuff. Then, we'll never be apart if you do it right, and you won't have to steal money from Mom. Isn't that great?"

Choking back a sob from anguish at what she was about to do, mixed with the thrill of hearing Colton's voice inside her mind again, Callie dropped to her knees.

"Yeah, that's it girl. Always knew you were kinky. Gonna call you Kinky Callie. Show me how bad you want it," De'Shawn whispered between moans. "Show me how bad you want to ease the pain."

Callie closed her eyes and focused on the prize instead of the humiliation, just like she learned to do while in pain when running.

5

CHAPTER FIVE

Graduation Night – Three Months Later

The gym decorations were fun and festive. Blue and gold streamers, bright lights, and countless balloons tied to the chairs transformed the space into a party zone. A pang of regret nearly made Callie gasp as the processional of students walked down the aisle. She wished her father was in the bleachers, sitting next to his wife watching yet another milestone of their children together. Looking over at the empty seat to the right, a lump of tears pressed against her throat. Someone had placed a card in the middle of the chair. In loopy cursive were the words *In honor of Colton Caleb Novak. Gone but never forgotten.*

"None of these fools cared about you when you were alive," Callie whispered while wiping a tear away.

"A few did. Wow, graduation. Remember how we used to dream about this day? How exciting the freedom of adulthood sounded?"

Colton's words were full of bitterness and regret. Hearing them made Callie feel the same. She couldn't stand to look at the card any longer. Snatching up the paper, she crushed it until nothing remained but a ball the size of a half-dollar. *Yes, I remember.*

The graduation committee went all out, determined to make the experience memorable. Kevin was part of the committee, and Callie wondered if the notecard was his idea.

While the speeches were given and applause thundered all around as each student's name was called, Callie's mind wandered. In a few months, she'd be in college, thanks to Ricky Weaver's help. Kevin had been right: Ricky was a math whiz, yet the boy was painfully shy. It took two weeks before he stopped blushing and stumbling over words and the real teaching started. Callie worked hard to understand the confusing equations, but when it came time to take tests, she went blank. At Ricky's urging, Callie turned in extra credit work and somehow managed to pass the class with a C—a grade she was grateful to get.

Determined not to get caught or arouse any suspicion, once Callie started dealing for De'Shawn, she only took pills at night. True to his word, De'Shawn gave her two baggies each month—one with product to be sold and the other crammed full of her personal stash. She forced herself to slow down on how many she took each night—cutting back to two at a time and only four on weekends after it dawned on her she could make extra cash by selling some of her own. She'd managed to squirrel away five hundred dollars and knew she'd be able to double, maybe triple that amount, in college. Before Christmas, she'd have enough to buy a cheap car. Callie had a host of regulars who bought from her, and she'd been surprised at the vastly different types of students who indulged.

Callie wasn't living the life she'd anticipated and meticulously planned for years, but she was making it, along with a strange cultural mix of new friends, which kept her occupied while Kevin and her mother worked. The connection with Colton strengthened during the past few months to the point she felt his presence all the time. Things at home weren't great, yet they were tolerable. The lawsuits were settled and talk of filing bankruptcy ceased. Once each week, Callie attended counseling sessions with her mother, rarely joining the discussion. Most of the time, when prodded for an answer, Callie gave short, simple responses then let the tears come.

She wouldn't say a friendship had developed between her and De'Shawn, but there was a weird sense of mutual admiration. He respected the fact Callie sold everything he gave her and never shorted him, always delivering the money promptly. Callie appreciated the fact he never prodded for sexual favors again.

When her name was called, Callie walked across the makeshift stage, pausing to smile for photos. The ceremony lasted less than two hours, and then everyone hugged each other, tears of joy, sadness, and excitement staining the faces of the majority of the student body.

Callie searched for Kevin, finally spying him in the crowd. He nodded and smiled, pointing to the parking lot. They'd planned out the entire evening, starting with a celebratory dinner with his family and her mom, followed by an evening at her house spent binge watching every "Star Wars" movie. Callie smiled, thinking how funny it was Kevin hated horror movies because of their unrealistic characters yet didn't see the same was true for sci-fi themed films.

The night would be boring but perfect. Callie wouldn't need any pills to sleep—the Force would lull her into slumber-land on its own.

Callie's purse buzzed, so she stepped away from the throng of students toward the bathroom. Extracting the cheap burner cell phone she'd purchased at Walmart, Callie flipped it open. Laughing while reading the text from a somewhat familiar number begging for some pills, Callie grinned. It would be the tenth sale of the day. She only had about twenty left. "At this rate, I'll be out of product before midnight! Guess people are ready to party after graduation!"

Meet me at the bus depot out back in 5 Callie texted back.

Stepping out into the gym once again, Callie searched for her mother. She spotted her talking with Kevin and his parents near the front entrance. After a quick gaze around the gym, searching for Coach Patterson, the grin spread as she watched him disappear out a side door. *Perfect cover!*

Pulling her regular cell, Callie sent a text to Kevin. *Be right back. Going to say goodbye to Coach P. Meet u at your car in 10.*

Watching to make sure Kevin received and read the text, she smiled and waved. He did, too, but for a fleeting moment, Callie noticed a strange look cross his face. While walking out to the bus depot, she wondered if the emotional impact of graduation was bothering him.

The big yellow buses sat in silence, all lined up in precise rows. Callie noticed a body leaning against the one furthest from the parking lot lights, though she couldn't make out whether it was male or female until about twenty yards away. When less than five feet apart, Callie's mouth dropped open from shock. "Ricky?"

"Hey, Callie. Surprised?"

"Beyond. All these months filling my brain with solutions to equations and you never said a word."

Ricky fidgeted from one foot to the next. Callie wondered if this was his first drug purchase.

"My aunt gave me a card with fifty dollars cash. Is that enough to get some hydrocodone pills?" Ricky asked.

"Something's wrong, Sis. Don't trust him."

Colton's voice made her feel uneasy. Callie took a step backward. Colton was right. The way Ricky asked was too formal—too tentative. "Who gave you the number?"

For a split second, the boy looked like a deer caught in headlights. The look wasn't unusual. Callie knew Ricky had a major crush on her, but something about his demeanor was off—weirder than normal.

Licking a set of thin lips, Ricky blinked twice. "I, uh, well, I asked Lisa Bowers, and she told me to fuck off. She, um, mentioned your name while walking away."

"That's bullshit," Colton whispered.

Callie's unease shifted to anger. Ever since she stopped buying pills from Lisa, the two hadn't spoken a peep to each other. "That doesn't explain how you got this number. Did you pilfer through my phone behind my back while tutoring me? Tell me the truth, or I'll lay you out right here. I'll give you enough pain you'll need Hydros for sure."

Ricky's gaze darted to the left at the same time Callie heard the sound of gravel crunching. Spinning around, assuming she was about to get jumped and possibly robbed, she froze. It took her mind a few seconds to produce a plausible story. "Kevin? Hey, look who I ran into? I was just thanking Ricky for—"

"Stop lying, Callie. I heard it all and recorded everything right here," Kevin said while holding his phone.

The look on his face and the shimmer of tears behind his beautiful eyes reinforced the words. The emotional pain of hurting the man she loved didn't last long. Rage at being set up overshadowed it. From behind her, the sound of Ricky scurrying away like a frightened rabbit sent waves of fury throughout Callie's chest. "You put him up to this, didn't you?"

"I did. And if you don't follow instructions, everyone will hear and see what I just did."

"You son-of-a-bitch!" Callie screamed, lunging for the phone.

"One more step and I'll post it everywhere…and send it to your mom."

Shaking with fury, Callie stepped back and glared at him. "What do you want from me?"

Pointing to the parking lot, Kevin answered, "Give me your purse and get in the car. Say anything else or try something stupid like attacking me again and you'll regret it."

Gripping her purse tighter, Callie yelled, "Traitor! How dare you try to control me like I'm something you own! Go ahead, post it. Tweet. Share. Text. I don't care what you do because we're done."

"You're wrong, Callie. If you don't get help, you're the one who's done."

Coach Patterson's stern voice broke through Callie's rage.

Turning, she faced him, shocked to see his eyes were glazed over with tears. "Did you just threaten me?"

"Callie...stop and think about who you're talking to and what you're saying to us! We love you and want you to get help! We've all suspected, but we knew without solid proof, you'd just keep lying to us. To yourself. Please, babe, get in the car and let us—"

"What?" Callie interrupted. "Take me to rehab? Is that your plan? If so, you've ruined graduation for nothing because there's no way I'm going."

"You will, or the Board of Directors at UALR will find a disturbing video in their inboxes on Monday morning, sent anonymously of course," Coach Patterson added.

"You'd really let him do that to me, Kevin? Take away my one shot at college? Ruin my life? I thought you loved me?" Callie gasped.

Stepping forward, Kevin looked her directly in the eyes. The amount of grief behind them made a lump of tears form in Callie's throat.

"If it means saving your life, yes. I do love you...always and forever. I'm willing to break my own heart to fix yours."

The words tore down the shields inside her heart. With a slight nod of agreement, she reached for Kevin's hand and let him lead her to his car, Coach Patterson only a few steps behind.

Hours later, the tears long gone after watching her mother and Kevin leave the rehabilitation facility, the first chill of fear slithered up Callie's spine. The fear mixed with simmering anger after glancing at the bag prepacked by her mother resting on the bench across the room. When Kevin pulled into the driveway and Coach Patterson followed them inside, Callie was stunned to find her mother, Dr. Brunson, and Mikki Taylor in the living room. They were like spiders ready to pounce on the unsuspecting meal caught in the sticky web. Mikki—the traitorous therapist—took the lead of the "intervention" as she called it, while everyone else nodded and cried.

Though she'd been furious, Callie knew she was trapped. Her angry, hateful words seemed to fall on deaf ears. No one budged from their stances, each pleading and begging Callie to seek treatment.

Callie refused, repeating she didn't have a problem, could stop anytime she wanted, and they were all crazy.

It wasn't until her mother fell to her knees, sobbing uncontrollably about how she'd die if something bad happened to her remaining child, Callie caved.

Mind still reeling from the events of the last four hours, Callie listened halfheartedly while the intake coordinator whose tag read simply "Sherry – Your partner at New Beginnings" asked question after question.

"How long and what kind of drugs do you use?"

"Xanax for about eight months; Vicodin close to four."

"When was last ingestion? Be honest, please."

Callie glanced up at the clock on the wall. *Way too long.* "About twelve hours."

"Any IV drug use?"

"Uh, no," Callie winced. "I'm not a junkie. That was my brother."

"Nice, Sis. Real nice," Colton shot back.

"Truth hurts, brother."

Sherry stopped writing, peering over the rim of her glasses. "Excuse me?"

"I, uh, nothing. Internal thought slipped out."

"You're aware we test the blood, not just urine, correct? To make sure we know exactly what's in your system and give you the right medication to help you during detoxification?"

Biting her nails too close to the nub, Callie grimaced as the taste of blood filled her mouth. "I'm in here for taking pills, yet the plan is to give me more to get off them? Makes perfect sense. Not."

Leaning forward, Sherry smiled. Rather than pleasant or kind, it was downright creepy. "When the withdrawals kick in, you'll be begging for the Naltrexone. Trust me. I've been in your shoes. Been clean now for six years. Detox is rough."

Sherry finally finished grilling Callie then excused herself to bring in a nurse to draw blood and take vital signs. Rubbing her arms, Callie closed her eyes and reached out to Colton. *I'm scared. I don't want to lose you again.*

"You won't, Sis. Just play their game. I'll help you, and before you know it, the thirty days will be over. Piece of cake. This little hiatus will give us plenty of time to dissect where you went wrong, how you got caught, and how to stay under the radar once you leave."

Then what?

Callie waited for the answer to whisper inside the corners of her mind. The silence made the tears come, along with the shakes. Anger rumbled inside her chest, making her skin tingle as it spread. People who claimed they cared betrayed her trust. Her love. The more she let the thoughts of their actions take over her mind, the anger continued to rise.

I'll do this to shut them up. I'll be truly free from prying eyes once in college. Truly free to live life the way I want.

6

CHAPTER SIX

Three Weeks Later

The noise level was ridiculous. The sounds of children yelling for attention competed with the voices of loved ones trying to converse with those they'd come to visit. The entire spectacle made Callie want to scream. She was already jittery and didn't need the added stress. The withdrawals, just like Sherry mentioned the first night she arrived, had been horrible during the first nine days. Thankfully, she'd finally stopped shaking and throwing up. Now, her biggest issues were insomnia and agitation.

She couldn't stand all the tears; the accusations hurled across the plastic tables; the heartbreak on the faces of both addicts and their loved ones. The interactions were pathetic at best, downright disturbing at worst. It was yet another reason she never added anyone's name to the visitation list. The thought of sitting in the cramped room, struggling to be heard over the racket while staring at the disappointed faces of her mother or Kevin made her skin crawl.

Turning, Callie headed back to her room. She made it halfway down the hall when Sherry called out her name. "Callie? A minute please?"

"I'm not feeling well. Can't it wait until later?"

"No, it can't. My office, please."

Gritting her teeth, Callie followed Sherry down the hall. *Just one more week. Just one more week and I'm out of here.*

Once inside the small, sparsely decorated room, Sherry pointed to the chair across from the desk. "Sit."

"Is there a problem?" Callie asked, sensing the tension in the room. "Is something wrong with my mother?"

"No, your mother is fine, considering things."

"What's that supposed to mean?"

"Considering her daughter's in rehab and refuses to see her, that's what."

Callie's temper flared. "You called me in here for that? You told me the night I came in it was my decision whether or not to have visitors, remember?"

"Yes, though most of our clients want to see a familiar face. You are a rarity."

"I've already explained why, Sherry. I don't want them here, seeing me like this. It's embarrassing."

Nodding, Sherry paused as though searching for the right words. "Is that your excuse as well for not sharing in group therapy and your insistence to not attend out-patient meetings once you're discharged? Embarrassment?"

Callie's anger intensified. "It's hard to get a word in since everyone else is sharing all their war stories. I don't see the therapeutic benefits of rehashing our past mistakes. It's almost like a freaking contest to see who has the worst story. And in terms of when I get out of here, I've already told you I have a therapist. Mikki Taylor, remember? I'll continue my weekly sessions with her."

"That's great, but it won't be enough. Sharing our troubles with others like us who understand our struggles allows us to look at who we were so we don't return to the lifestyle, Callie. It's called—"

"Lancing the wounds. Yes, I know. Great expression, by the way, that seems to work wonders. The people who've been in here four, five, even six times are proof."

"It does work if you follow the program, take the right steps when outside, learn to avoid triggers," Sherry responded.

"Look, Sherry, I'm not like those people out there! Those are hardcore meth heads, junkies, and God only knows what other drugs! Most of them are here because the courts forced them to seek treatment. Some have lost custody of their kids! One girl even sold her two-year-old daughter for a week's worth of heroin! I'm just a normal girl who got injured playing sports and found out I liked the way the Vicodin made me feel. End of story. I'm clean now and won't go back to using. I have nothing in common with them!"

A spark of anger flared behind Sherry's dark eyes. Callie felt the electricity level in the room rise.

"You're wrong, Callie. The common thread is all of you are addicts. The type of drug isn't the connecting link—the behavior is. Lying to those who love you; hiding your addiction and doing things you never thought you could be capable of just to get high. You didn't care about the feelings of those around you or yourself. Plus, you didn't just use drugs. You stooped to the level of selling, too. What if someone who bought from you overdosed and died? I bet—no, I know—you didn't even think about that. All you cared about was making enough money to buy more."

"Whatever," Callie muttered.

"I assume you had a dealer you bought from?"

Callie said nothing.

"Uh-huh, thought so. You made him or her a lot of money. Once you leave here, they'll show up, wanting to know if you ratted them out, and if you're lucky enough to convince them you didn't, they'll push you to start selling again. That scenario isn't an if one—it's a when. How are you going to handle that? Do you really think thirty days in here has made you strong enough to walk away?"

Callie refused to answer. Instead, she stared at the floor.

"You're a dual threat—addict and dealer. In other words, you are just like everyone else here, so stop deluding yourself. Now, as I've mentioned many times in group, we insist on honesty from all our clients. Ready to tell me the truth?"

Again, Callie remained quiet even though it was a struggle. A thousand nasty comebacks danced on the tip of her tongue.

"Your injury was only a few months ago. Xanax isn't a painkiller as you well know. Based on what I've read in your file, you started not long after the death of your brother and father. Look how fast your life changed once you started getting high."

The anger turned to rage. Callie stood, shoving the chair back so hard it crashed into the gray wall. "I've told you before I will *not* talk about their deaths! I won't!"

"You loved them both very much, that's easy to see. Emotional upheaval is a common trigger point in addicts. We don't handle the stressors of life very well. Instead, we seek out something to numb our pain."

"See? Once again, you're way off base. You think you know me and understand my motivations? You're wrong."

"How so?" Sherry queried.

"I started using to reconnect—" Callie clamped her mouth shut, realizing she'd just walked into Sherry's trap.

"I understand Colton was your fraternal twin."

Callie nodded, angry at letting her real emotions slip out. She'd been careful to keep them hidden the past three weeks during group and individual therapy.

"I've heard identical twins share strong bonds, sometimes feeling each other's pain, or they possess the uncanny ability to know what the other is thinking. Is that true with fraternal twins, too?"

Unable to look Sherry in the eyes, Callie stared out the window. Tufts of white, fluffy clouds rolled by, revealing the brilliant blue sky. It was close to the same color as the butterfly on her foot.

"Yes," Callie whispered.

"You were close to your father but shared something really special with your brother. The loss was too much to handle."

Sherry's words were a statement rather than a question. Callie hated the fact the woman had the ability to see right into her heart. Hearing another person say them made the pain all the more real. "I miss him so much. Everything I did—all my achievements—they weren't for me. They were for him! Colton was gifted. He drew and painted such stunning work. His life was over before it really started."

"And you feel guilty because you're still here and he isn't. Right?" Sherry pressed.

Warm tears slid down Callie's cheeks. "No, I feel guilty because I knew something was wrong—I suspected he was doing more than Xanax, but I ignored it! I was too wrapped up in trying to make the future brighter for him that I lost sight of the present. I'm angry at the same time, which makes no sense. I'm so angry at Colton for dying…for killing our dad and breaking Mom's heart. Yet, more than anything, I'm scared because the connection we had is gone. It's like I've been wandering around in the dark, only able to see when his light comes back."

"What do you mean?"

Callie had never spoken her true feelings out loud, not even to Mikki or Kevin. The enormity of the emotions made her sob. "My mom gave me a Xanax one night without telling me. When I realized what she'd done the next day, I was furious. We had a huge fight. I was really mad at her but at the same time, almost grateful, because Colton came to me. Inside my head, not like a ghost or something. The connection was back. Not the same or as strong, but back. Then, when I got hurt and started taking the Vicos, well, I don't know how to explain it. I felt whole again."

Sherry's brow furrowed with worry. "You're saying you started using because your brother—your dead brother—urged you to?"

"I know, sounds crazy, but it's the truth. I felt him! Saw his face inside my mind. We talked all the time! It was amazing. But, ever since I've been here, I can't feel or talk to him anymore, and it's tearing me apart."

Sherry rose from the chair and walked over to Callie, placing a warm hand on her shoulder. "Did he encourage you to use, or was he upset about it?"

Wiping the wetness from her face, Callie whispered, "Urged."

"Oh, Callie! Don't you see? If it was really your brother talking to you, he would've been urging you to stay strong! He died because of drug use and kept his addiction a secret. If he really thought it was okay for you to walk down this path, he would've said something to you while still alive, but he didn't. The voice inside your mind wasn't your brother. It's the monster we know as addiction. It roared to life after your first taste of drugs! People who love us and truly have our best interests at heart don't encourage us to do something that is so detrimental to our health."

The tears came faster. Callie collapsed on the floor, sobbing. "You're wrong, Sherry. It was Colton. He just needed me to help him. He's all alone!"

"Callie, he's gone. Departed from this world forever. I don't know what you believe about life after death, but I do believe the soul—our essence if you will—continues on. Colton loved you, so why in the world do you think he'd guide you down this path? Look where you are! You weren't just using drugs but dealing them as well. Honestly, do you think that's the life he wanted you to lead?"

The sobs lessened as the anger from before resurfaced. "I didn't come here because I wanted to, Sherry. I was forced—given no choice! Betrayed by those who love me, so which is worse? The actions of the living or the dead?"

"Stop blaming others for your decisions, Callie. That's the first step to recovery! You made the choices, good and bad, in your life. Take responsibility for them and learn new ways of coping with the grief. The path you're on now only ends in one of three ways: prison, the streets, or death."

"You don't know that, Sherry," Callie answered.

"Wrong. Years of experience with addicts, and being one myself, back me up. I do agree with one thing you said though, and again, years of experience prove my point."

"And that is?"

"You aren't broken. Until you, as the expression goes, hit rock bottom, you're just wasting everyone's time here, yourself included. Until you're ready to admit you have a problem and truly want to fight this disease, you'll continue to use."

Callie brushed off Sherry's hand and stood, furious at the callous words. "Like I said earlier, you don't know me and have no right to judge me. One more week and then I'm out of here, and I promise, you'll never see my face again."

With that, Callie stormed out of Sherry's office, ignoring the others milling around in the hallway. Once inside her room, she slammed the door, fuming. *I'll prove you wrong, Sherry. I'll prove all of you wrong. Mark my words.*

7

CHAPTER SEVEN

Six Weeks Later

"Callie? I'm home."

"Be down in a minute, Mom. Just got out of the shower," Callie yelled back, wondering why her mother was home so early.

While dressing, she couldn't help but smile. Once her mother stepped into the kitchen, she'd be surprised to see Callie had fixed dinner and set the table. Ever since coming home from rehab, Callie tried to make up for all the drama and pain she'd caused. Making amends gave her something to do—to think about—when the cravings kicked in, or when missing Colton became too much to handle.

Looking at life through sober eyes opened her mind up to really see how frail her mother had become. In a little over a year, Annie Novak had aged way too fast. The few gray hairs had multiplied and now her headful of lovely blonde hair was almost all white. Dark circles rimmed her eyes no matter how much concealer she put on. Deep worry lines creased her forehead, eyes, and around her mouth. Callie hated the fact some of the changes were her fault.

They'd had several heart-to-heart talks in therapy, saving the real gut-wrenching discussions for home. Each really bared their souls and truly talked about the emotional impact of losing the two men in their lives. The only thing Callie lied about was where she'd gotten the pills. She couldn't bring herself to tell her mother all the times she'd been out running at night wasn't at the track. Her mother would have a heart attack or stroke if she knew Callie had been running across town over to the "hood" and buying drugs from a street thug. Instead, she continued to let her mother think she'd gotten the pills from other kids at school.

Callie apologized for what she'd done, and her mother did the same, breaking down at the kitchen table after an intense counseling session with Mikki, begging for forgiveness for giving Callie Xanax on the sly.

The weeks had been difficult yet certainly better than rehab. Her cell phone was shut off and the burner phone long gone. She was glad she'd never texted or called De'Shawn from the number. The thought of anyone connecting her with him made her shudder. Someone—her mother she assumed—found her stash of money under the bed and had taken it. Colton's voice inside her mind stopped talking, and though she hated to admit it, Sherry was right: it wasn't really him. Though she missed him, she was learning to live each day without his presence.

The first month was awful since she had a wicked case of insomnia. Once she started running again two weeks ago, it helped, but not much. When she did manage to sleep, she was plagued with horrible nightmares. She'd basically been a hermit, rarely leaving the house, spending each day exercising to the point of collapsing. Another new obsession was learning to cook. For some odd reason, throwing ingredients together, creating something worth eating, gave Callie a sense of accomplishment.

The only big issue Callie hadn't addressed was her relationship with Kevin. She was still angry at him for what he'd done—the ways he betrayed her—and refused to take his calls or see him when he came to visit the first week she came home. The way she figured, they were over. Too much damage had been done. Neither one would ever trust the other again. Besides, school would start soon, which meant time and distance apart. It was best to just let the relationship fizzle out as they grew up and apart, rather than have some wicked showdown and things get ugly.

"Bullshit. I'm just afraid to face him," Callie whispered while yanking on a t-shirt. "I don't want to see the distrust and sadness in another set of eyes. The pain in Mom's is bad enough. God, if he were to ever suspect about what happened between me and De'Shawn—how I cheated on him—I'd just die. He's better off without me anyway."

Shaking the thoughts away, Callie pulled her long hair into a ponytail then bounded down the stairs. She couldn't wait to tell her mother the good news. When she entered the kitchen, her mom was at the table, eyes clouded over with tears.

"You're crying already? You haven't even tasted the food yet! I promise I followed your recipes," Callie said, laughing. "I expected you to be shocked, not crying!"

"It's just so sweet of you, honey. And I'm not crying. These are just a few tears of happiness."

Callie took the roast and potatoes out of the oven while her mother scooped out salad and buttered cornbread. Once back at the table, Callie noticed her mom was really pale. "Are you okay, Mom?"

"I'm fine. I just had a rough day at work. Mmm, the roast is really good. So, tell me why you made all my favorites."

"Am I that transparent?" Callie laughed.

"Sometimes."

Callie let the veiled dig slide. "I can't help it. I'm just so excited. Guess what?"

"You talked to Kevin today?"

A spark of hope glimmered behind her mother's weary blue eyes. "Mom…we agreed no talking about Kevin. This is about me. I got a job today!"

"You did? That's wonderful! Where?"

"The bookstore at UALR. I applied online."

"You did? And here I thought you hated technology."

"I've got to learn before college starts, right?" Callie laughed. "Anyway, they called me less than an hour later. Had a phone interview and everything! I have to go and meet with the manager tonight at six. He's leaving to go on vacation tomorrow and will be gone for a week, so may I take the car?"

The look of instant distrust and doubt on her mother's face made Callie tense. *God, how much longer will it be before she stops looking at me like that?*

"At six? Isn't that kind of an odd time for an interview?"

It took a few seconds to steady herself so she didn't sound irritated. "I already told you why, Mom. Look, I understand you have no reason to trust me. Really. So how about you drive me over there and see for yourself? Okay?"

"Mighty grownup of you, dear. I'm sorry. I *am* trying. It's just difficult sometimes. I imagine I'll be a basket case when you leave for school."

The kitchen fell silent as they both picked at their food. Callie's appetite disappeared and so, it seemed, did her mother's. Callie decided to change the subject. "Is today a holiday or something?"

"What?"

"You're home early. Why?"

"Oh, well, we've been slow, so my boss let me go early. He said it's normal for business to slack off during the summer. People go on vacation and such."

Studying her mother's drawn and tired face, Callie noticed she was gritting her jaw—a habit she did when lying. "Mikki says we are to tell each other the truth, Mom."

A few tears raced down her mother's cheeks before she had the chance to wipe them away. "It's nothing, CeeCee. I just got my hours cut back, that's all."

"Oh, Mom. I'm sorry. Maybe you should start looking for a new job? You know, one that pays better and where your boss treats you with respect and not like a work horse?"

"I will. Now that's enough about me. Let's finish this wonderful meal and then we'll head over to UALR. Maybe get some ice cream from Baskin Robbins on the way back? Just like old times?"

"Sounds perfect. And don't worry, Mom. Everything will be okay from now on. I promise."

"Look! I'm officially employed!" Callie squealed after jumping into the passenger seat. She waved the forms her new boss gave her to fill out and bring back Wednesday.

"That's wonderful, honey! Did you find out what hours you'll be working? We need to know so we can schedule accordingly."

"Wednesday through Friday will be from four p.m. until eight p.m., every Saturday four to midnight. I start this coming Wednesday, but don't worry! It's only what, five miles from the house? I'll just run until move-in day on campus. I need to step up training anyway."

Putting the car in drive, her mother pulled out of the parking lot. "No you won't. No way. Too dangerous, especially working that late. Until you move in, we'll share the car. I won't have you running these streets on foot at midnight. Guess it's a good thing my hours were cut back, huh?"

Smiling, Callie answered, "Temporarily, yes. But the minute I move onto campus, you go find a great job and tell your boss to kiss your ass."

"Callie Claire!"

"Sorry, Mom. So, when we get home, will you help me with these forms? I don't want to screw them up."

"Of course, baby. But first we must have ice cream! Mint chocolate chip here we come!"

All ready for her first day at work after changing outfits three different times, Callie paced back and forth in the living room waiting for her mother to arrive home. She picked and nipped at the skin around her nails, making them bleed—a new habit she developed in rehab.

Peeking at the window when she heard a car, she let out a sigh of relief and ran outside.

"Sorry I'm late. Bad traffic," her mother said while exiting the car. "Had to stop and get you something to mark the day."

Callie gasped when her mother produced her old cell phone. "Oh, Mom. Thank you."

"Don't get too excited now. It's on a limited plan—250 minutes each month and less than a gig of data. It's just for emergencies. I want you to be safe when at school and the parking lot at night."

Swallowing a lump of tears, Callie nodded.

"This is a month-to-month plan, and I expect you to pay it, okay? No freebie, no enabling, like Mikki said. You've got a job now, so it'll be your responsibility. Now, I'm really tired honey so why don't you just drive? You'll be home by eight-fifteen, right?"

Callie smiled. It would be the first time in months she'd been able to drive alone and have access to a phone other than the land line! "Thanks, Mom. Dinner's in the microwave, and yes, I'll come home right after work. Promise."

Climbing behind the wheel, Callie waved goodbye and drove to UALR, thrilled her life was finally changing for the better, and the trust she desperately wanted to regrow with her mother finally started to bloom.

"Great job tonight, Callie. You picked up on things really quick, just like we all thought. See you tomorrow."

"Thanks, Stephanie. You're a good teacher."

"Not like there's a whole lot to learn here," Stephanie replied, laughing, her wide, green eyes full of playfulness. "The best part is helping out the hunky athletes who come in here clueless and in need of assistance. Eye candy!"

Callie laughed. "I'll be too busy studying and training to pay attention."

Raising an eyebrow, Stephanie teased, "If you're worried your boyfriend might get jealous, don't. They don't care what gets our motors running just as long as they run! Mine knows when I've had interactions with some sexy jock because I ride him like a bull!"

"Wow, a bit of TMI there, Stephanie," Callie responded. "Thanks for the laugh, but I've got to go. See you tomorrow night."

"Be careful in the parking lot. Creepers. Want to wait until nine when I close up? We can walk out together."

"I've got to get home, sorry. I'll be fine. Thanks, though."

Callie left the library and headed to the car at the far end of the lot. The last rays of the orange sun streaked across the sky, making the clouds look almost like cotton candy. While walking, her thoughts wandered over to Kevin. Hearing Stephanie talk about her boyfriend made Callie want to see him. Not for sex, but just to talk and hash things out. Let the relationship end on a good note rather than a bad one.

She stopped in mid-stride, pulling out the cell phone from her purse. Her hands shook while tapping out a text. *Got a job that I applied for online all by myself you were a good teacher call me around 8:30?*

"You really should pay more attention to your surroundings, Kinky. Haven't you heard parking lots are dangerous places for women?"

The sound of De'Shawn's ominous voice from behind her made Callie's heart pound. The car was a good fifty yards away and there wasn't a soul in the parking lot besides the two of them. She could run, but it was doubtful she'd unlock the car and make it inside before he reached her. *God, Sherry was right!*

Instead of turning to face him, Callie squared her shoulders and kept walking. "What are you doing here, De'Shawn?"

He picked up his pace, pulling even. "I've missed you, Kinky. Well, actually not you, just the money. Heard you went to rehab and got all squeaky clean. You didn't break down and tell anyone about our business transactions, did you?"

"Did the cops come knocking?" Callie shot back, praying as she neared the car. De'Shawn produced a sick, twisted grin while shaking his head. "Then there's your answer."

In a flash, he was in front of her, blocking her path to the car. "Always knew you were a smart girl. Now, we wouldn't want anything bad to happen to your mom or that nerd you call a boyfriend, or shall I say *used* to call a boyfriend. They'll be just fine if you play by my rules."

She knew it was a dangerous choice to let the anger erupt, but Callie was unable to stop herself. "Don't you dare threaten me or anyone I love, you bastard. I never said one word to a soul about where I got the pills from, but I swear to God, if you try—"

Before she could blink, De'Shawn lunged, grabbing her around the throat. The impact of her body slamming into the side of the car made stars appear. "Shut up and listen, bitch. You don't run the show. I do. You work for me, remember? There's plenty of money to be made here—way more than you can imagine. I want my part of the pie here on campus. I don't give a shit if you use pills or not, but you will sell them for me."

"I won't," Callie hissed, her hands clawing and scratching at De'Shawn's face.

Squeezing harder, De'Shawn answered, "You will, or you'll be attending more funerals. The five-hundred dollars I found in your room took care of what you owed me, but I want more."

He let go and Callie's body collapsed onto the warm pavement, purse, keys, and cell phone flying. She heard the tinkle of glass and knew the phone was toast. Gasping for air, stunned he'd been inside her bedroom, she couldn't stop him when he grabbed her purse and shoved a wrinkled paper sack inside.

"Welcome back, Kinky. God, how I enjoy doing business with you!"

De'Shawn took off, running across the parking lot. In seconds, his body disappeared into a clump of trees. Crawling on all fours, Callie scooped up her purse and keys. Once inside the car, her hands shook so hard she couldn't insert the key.

"Okay, breathe. He's gone," Callie whispered. "He's gone."

She opened the sack and sure enough, two large plastic bags crammed with white pills rested inside. The terror disappeared, replaced with white-hot fury. Grabbing them, she rolled down the window, intent on tossing them out, yet she didn't.

De'Shawn had obviously been keeping an eye on her or how else would he have known where she worked? Knowing he'd been inside her house made the hairs stand up all over her body. She'd steered clear of all social media since coming out of rehab, and no one but her mother and the employees of the bookstore knew her schedule. The only logical conclusion was he'd been following her or had others keeping tabs on her whereabouts.

That part was bad enough, but the threats against her mother and Kevin—the thought was so disturbing Callie opened the driver's door and threw up.

"Okay, get it together. I can't go home like this, all freaked out. I can't tell a soul what just happened. Just get home before Mom starts worrying. Deal with this mess later."

Callie started up the car and pulled out onto University Avenue. She glanced at the clock, wincing at the time. It was 8:20, and she had no way to call her mother since her phone was busted.

While driving home, Callie prayed her mother had fallen asleep on the couch as she'd been doing for the last few weeks so she wouldn't see the terror and fear on her daughter's face.

Instead of parking in the driveway, Callie pulled up to the curb and turned the car off. Glancing at the house, she noticed the only light was from the back porch. Grabbing her purse and keys, Callie closed the door with a gentle push, hoping her mother was on the phone out back and didn't hear her pull up. It would give her enough time to sneak inside, hit the shower, hide the drugs, and calm down before lying to her mother about what happened at her first day at work.

"Lying. Again. Shit. At least this time I have a good reason," Callie muttered while walking up the driveway.

By the time she reached the side of the garage, she heard the sound of her mother crying. The noise sent Callie into a tailspin, fearful De'Shawn had already stopped by.

"How am I supposed to tell her, Kevin? How? Addicts don't deal well with change!"

The words stopped her from bursting through the gate at the side of the house. Instead of running, Callie crept forward until only inches from the fence. *She's talking to Kevin? What? Why?*

"I don't know yet. I'm looking at some apartments near campus. I'm aware that's a bad area, but there really isn't much choice. There's simply no money left, and I can only afford so much. Yes, uh-huh. We've got twenty days to leave. Would you? That would be wonderful. You're such an amazing person, Kevin. Thank you."

Callie heard enough. Rather than crying, she turned and ran to the front door, taking the stairs two-at-a-time. Once inside her room, she stuffed the pills in the back of her closet inside an old tampon box and then jumped into the shower.

The hot water did nothing to calm her stressed-out mind as she replayed back the snippets of what she'd overheard, along with the disastrous confrontation with De'Shawn. No matter how hard she scrubbed, she couldn't wash away the stench of her fears. The conclusions made her chest tighten: her mother's financial woes were much worse than she realized, and Callie was screwed.

"Honey?"

A sense of paranoia made Callie's heart thunder inside her chest, knowing her mother was only feet away from the stash of pills. "Be out in a minute, Mom. I had to take a shower. I smelled like stale books."

"Come downstairs when you're done and tell me about your day. Okay?"

"Sure thing."

After drying off, Callie tossed on her favorite pajamas then stared at herself in the mirror. The reflection was the same on the outside, but the girl on the inside was a totally different story. She started shaking as the weight of the situation soaked in. "No, not now. Freak later. Go find out what's really going on before jumping to conclusions."

Callie left the bathroom and headed downstairs.

"In here, baby."

Callie veered left and went to the kitchen. Her mother stood at the sink, staring out the window with a sad, strange look on her face. "What's wrong, Mom? It looks like you've been crying."

Nodding once and pointing to the table, she sat, waiting for Callie to do the same. "Yes, and it's time I tell you why. Before I do, I'd like to hear about your first day."

"No, Mom. Spill. What's going on?"

For the next twenty minutes, Callie listened in stunned silence while her mother talked. The house payments were too much to handle, she'd been unable to refinance, and the income from her job wasn't enough. The foreclosure papers were served ten days prior, and they had to be out at the end of the month. On top of everything else, she'd been let go from her job.

"The official reason was lack of work, but a co-worker called me after I left today and said it was because the insurance premiums went up. I'm so sorry, honey. I know this is a lot to take in at one time—"

"Wait," Callie interrupted. "I don't understand the insurance part. Why did the premiums go up?"

Looking away, her mother didn't answer. It took Callie a few minutes to put the pieces of the confusing puzzle together. "The premiums went up because of me, didn't they? My trip to rehab?"

Tears sprang from her mother's eyes, dripping onto the table. She didn't move, didn't speak, but the destroyed look on her face was answer enough.

Callie didn't know what to say or do. Thoughts barreled through her mind at a dizzying pace. There was too much to think about; too much to stress over.

Too much humiliation and shame.

"Kevin offered to come over and help us pack. Please don't be upset, but I've been talking to him. He's been so worried about you, and it didn't feel right to leave him in the dark. He loves you so much."

The words seemed muffled and distant, as though they'd floated in the window from miles away, overshadowed by the crazy thoughts swirling inside her mind.

Kevin.

The house.

De'Shawn.

Dealing again.

Moving.

Her mother's pain.

In a dull monotone, Callie said, "I'm not mad, Mom. Whatever we need to do to get through this, we will."

"Thank you, baby."

"It's been quite a day for both of us. Let's call it a night and tackle these issues tomorrow, after a good night's rest."

Rising from the chair, her mother nodded in agreement. "Good idea. I'm exhausted. See you in the morning, sweetheart."

On autopilot, Callie followed her mother upstairs. They kissed each other goodnight and headed to their rooms. Unable to sleep, Callie paced around, biting every single nail down to the quick. She felt like a caged animal unable to breathe, so she climbed out onto the roof. Even though the evening air was humid and hot, she didn't care. She had to get outside the crushing walls.

"What am I going to do?" Callie whispered to the sparkling stars and ebony sky. "How can this be happening? Why do you hate me, God?"

The tears arrived, pouring out of her with each heave of her chest. The mental pain was more than she could stand. It felt like something had reached inside her soul, ripping and shredding it to pieces, and she knew only one way to make it stop.

Callie stopped crying and went back inside, heading straight to the bathroom. *Just one. Just for tonight. I've got to rest before my mind explodes.*

8

CHAPTER EIGHT

Present Day

The memory of the night she caved and started taking pills again made Callie shake her head. She hated reliving past mistakes, but at least they weren't as bad as the intense cravings during the past three days. Those had almost driven her to the point of madness. They'd plagued her nonstop while suffering through horrific withdrawals. She wouldn't dare set foot into any sort of rehab facility since she was on the run, fearing questions about her identity might be asked. Rather than risk getting picked up and sent back to Arkansas to prison, Callie chose to beat the monster on her own, using the tools she'd learned at *New Beginnings* to see her through the nightmare.

Of course, this was the first time she'd attempted coming off heroin. She knew it was a dangerous choice to do on her own after witnessing a few poor souls go through it in rehab. The time Callie was forced to sober up before had been from pills. She'd been a fool to think the experience with dope would be similar. Big H was a different monster—one with stronger teeth and a bigger bite that fought back hard when trying to slay it.

The shakes, seizing muscles, and violent bouts of vomiting left her mind dazed and body weak. She'd spent the last seventy-two-plus hours alternating between puking in the bathroom, crying on the bed, and then to sitting in the shower until the water ran cold.

She'd endured three days of Hell on earth inside the one-room duplex.

Alone.

So, when day four of trying to remain sober started out rather uneventfully, Callie was thrilled. After a few hours of restless sleep dreaming about the past, she'd shuffled to the kitchen, fixed some unbuttered toast, and managed to keep it down along with tepid coffee. It was the first time in a nearly a week she had the mental clarity and strength to contemplate getting cleaned up to head back to work.

"Work—what a joke! Selling my body certainly wasn't what I wanted to do for a living," Callie muttered while swallowing the last drops of coffee. "Like Teri always said, hooking is the worst kind of job around—writhing on random kooks. Can I even do it anymore when sober? Ugh, doubtful."

Cooler weather and hordes of football fans and players in town meant she was missing out on some prime money. Sidestepping the trash strewn across the cracked linoleum floor, Callie walked over to the counter and opened her wallet. After counting the cash inside, she nixed the idea of trolling for johns. Enough green was stuffed inside to pay the rent on the hovel plus the light bill.

Once the bills were paid for the month, it would leave her with less than two bucks, which wasn't enough to buy a hit. Besides, her decision to quit cold turkey stemmed from the brutal beating she'd received a little over one week ago, coupled with Teri's death.

The memory of waking up in a back alleyway crammed next to a dumpster, battered, bloody, and sore, made Callie shiver. She still couldn't believe she'd survived.

Teri wasn't so fortunate.

Recalling when she touched Teri's stiff, cold hand, made the toast and coffee threaten to come back up. She'd panicked in those wee hours of the predawn after realizing Teri was dead, a needle stuck in her arm.

The john who picked them up enjoyed hurting Callie more because she fought back once she realized they were in danger. When Callie intervened and tried to stop the bastard from tying Teri up, all hell broke loose. The man attacked Callie without mercy, never saying a word as he pummeled her face, chest, stomach, and back until she passed out.

The sleazebag client seemed fascinated by taking bondage to a whole new level. When he'd finally satiated himself, he'd tossed them out of his car in the dead of night. Callie could barely walk, so Teri pulled her into an alleyway, insisting they hide behind a dumpster until Callie rested up enough to make it home.

"We can't just go walking down the street with you looking so rough. Hell, you can barely walk! Someone would call the cops!" Teri had whispered. "I ain't going back to jail for nothing or nobody…not even for you, KiKi. Done had my fill of being caged like a rabid dog."

The last thing Callie remembered before passing out again was Teri crying, mumbling about how no one had ever done something so nice for her before and how she didn't like it one bit. "I ain't gonna be owing anyone a thing. I ain't!"

Callie wondered if Teri overdosed on purpose or by accident.

When Callie woke up—still high and minus a roommate—she did the unthinkable: she rolled her only friend and took all Teri's cash, her ID, and the small baggie of dope inside her purse. She left Teri "Sugar Beets" Cantrell alone on the ground to be discovered by a stranger. When found, Teri would be just another statistic—another nameless, dead junkie whore whose life ended in a dirty alley on the bad side of the tracks in Memphis. She'd only glanced back once at the lifeless body of the woman who'd taken her in from the streets, showed her how to turn tricks without being controlled by some brutal pimp, and introduced her to the world of smack.

Callie grit her teeth as Teri's words replayed inside her head from the first night she spent inside the duplex. "The pills you like are hard to get on the streets, KiKi. This ain't the 'burbs, honey. No parents around with medicine cabinets full of Xanax or Hydros. Government's done cracked down hard on pharmacies. Don't you worry, honey. I've got something better and cheaper to keep you straight, and there's plenty of it around. Makes the jobs a breeze and takes the edge off a tired mind. You can stay here as long as you pay half the rent, utilities, and groceries. Oh, and help out on occasion with Simon. He's the landlord. He's gonna love you."

The words—spoken less than eight months ago—changed Callie's life. Strung out, beyond desperate for a release from the mental torture inside her mind, Callie let Teri introduce her to the poison that killed Colton.

The rush, the warmth, the overwhelming sense of euphoria quieting her mind took Callie's life to a whole new level. She went from a pill head to a full-blown heroin addict seconds after her first taste of the mind-numbing bliss.

Callie shook her head to rid herself of the memories while walking to the kitchen. Rummaging through the small fridge and cabinets, she took inventory of what remained. Though not much, it didn't matter. She never ate regular meals anyway. The remaining items should last at least another week.

Smiling at her resolve to stay off the streets another night, Callie settled onto the couch to watch the sunset. Seeing the vivid oranges, pinks, yellows, and hints of blue bounce off the glass and concrete of the tall buildings downtown reminded her of Colton. God, how much her twin loved to sit on the rooftop, hands flying across the canvas while recreating the images from the sky with paint!

Thinking about Colton made her heart pound and led to thoughts of the rest of her non-existent family and friends. She didn't think about them when the heroin train took over the tracks inside her mind, which is exactly why she let the dark horse be conductor. However, after thinking about him, Callie yearned to see his face or hear his voice again. Ever since the first prick of the needle, he'd been silent. Sherry had been right on the money—the voice inside her mind she wanted to believe was her dead brother was addiction, and once she truly let it control her life, she didn't need the voice to urge her on.

Antsy and unable to sit still, she made the mistake of looking through the flimsy photo album hidden under piles of clothes and garbage next to the couch. The photos were all aged, yellowed pictures of the life she'd once led. The photo album, along with Colton's journal and drawing pad, were the only things she'd grabbed from home after stealing the wad of cash her mother kept hidden in the closet for emergencies.

While Callie flipped through the album crammed with smiling faces of her parents holding their twins at various stages of development, a cheesy grin plastered across their faces in every shot, her chest tightened.

Home.

Mom, with her long, blonde hair and lithe frame, beautiful blue eyes always full of playfulness when a camera came near.

Dad, Callie's hero and biggest fan. Always cheering her on, waiting at the finish line with a huge smile and big hug.

Colton—a mirror image of Callie with shorter hair—a boy with a brilliant, creative mind and loving soul.

Benny, their enormous, slobbering St. Bernard with a ball in his mouth in almost every picture.

The grainy photo of Callie and Colton waving to the camera while sitting in the little plastic pool on a hot summer day when they were around six made the tears come. Callie gasped at the one of all four of them in front of their new home in the suburbs, complete with a large backyard sporting an in-ground swimming pool and a playset big enough for all the neighborhood kids to play on. God, how happy they'd all been the day of the move-in, and how utterly devastated the two remaining Novaks had been when they moved out.

It seemed like eons ago.

No, it seemed like someone else's life.

As she neared the back pages, the photos were replaced with paper certificates. Colton won award after award for his paintings—he'd been the creative one of the pair. Callie's were all from track and volleyball achievements since she'd been the athlete.

The scholarship letter from UALR made her cringe with regret.

The picture of the senior prom with Kevin made her shake with sorrow.

The last page was the obituary notice, informing the prying eyes of the world that Joseph Jeffrey Novak and Colton Caleb Novak died in a car accident, leaving a beloved wife and cherished child behind.

The memories sent Callie—nicknamed Kinky Kayla by her regulars—into a tailspin.

The urge to let her mind slip away into warm, tranquil obscurity revved up, so Callie tried everything she could think of to stop it. Stuffing the photo album behind the couch, she ignored the scurry of roaches skittering across the dirty floor. Lacing up her old track shoes, Callie stepped out into the approaching night, running through the damp streets until collapsing from exhaustion.

The mental anguish of knowing her physical stamina and strength had diminished so rapidly in such a short time made her chest heavy with remorse. During her junior year of high school, before the descent into madness with pills began, Callie ran 1600 meters in five minutes.

Not anymore.

Not even close.

Another piece of her life destroyed by hard living and even harder drugs.

Callie limped down the dirty side street, tears running down her face.

After heating up some ramen noodles, Callie tried reading a book. Squinting at the pages made her eyes hurt, so she popped in a DVD of *The Princess Bride*. She'd stolen it from a convenience store shelf weeks ago. It was her favorite movie and reminded her of home. When she was little, her father told her she'd grow up to look just like Buttercup, laughing when four-year-old Callie said "Butterfly" instead of Buttercup.

Looking down, Callie winced. The blue butterfly tattoo on her foot had been the source of numerous arguments with her mother about "permanently defacing" her body.

"God, a clean mind is an ugly place full of tormenting memories," Callie whispered.

She was dying for a hit and wished there was someone to call—a friend, a sponsor, or even a fellow addict trying to stay clean.

Someone.

Anyone.

Addiction destroyed all her previous relationships, leaving Callie alone in a dark, evil world full of users. Even if a single person from her old life still cared about her, she wouldn't risk a call. Callie feared the connection might lead to her arrest, so the burner cell phone remained on the counter, untouched.

The hunger gained momentum, controlled every thought, sparking every nerve ending. Pacing back and forth like a trapped, wild beast inside the confines of the filthy, sparsely furnished duplex, Callie was full of regret and remorse. She hated herself for being born, hated Colton for killing himself and their dad, hated her mother for being a pill head—and turning Callie into one.

She hated the cruel, ugly world she was trapped in, allowing sick, demented strangers to do unspeakable things to her body just so she could get high.

"What have I done to myself? How in the world did this happen to me?" Callie whimpered to the silent four walls.

The shakes set in, followed by sweat soaking her dirty t-shirt and shorts in seconds. The rank odor of perspiration mixed with the strong aroma of the unkempt space made her feel queasy.

Callie missed her mom—needed her more than ever and would give anything to hear her voice again.

She wasn't available to help, and never would be again.

Annie Marie Novak was dead, her life cut short when a massive coronary stopped her heart. One week before last Christmas, Callie was to appear in front of Judge Hershel and plead guilty to numerous charges, including possession of Schedule II narcotics with intent to deliver and public intoxication after being arrested on campus. The plea deal, worked out by a public defender, would send Callie to prison for one year. When they pulled into the parking lot of the courthouse, the news about her remaining child's future was just too much for Annie Novak to accept.

When her mother's body crumpled onto the pavement in the parking lot, Callie fled, using the ensuing chaos as a chance to escape. The moment was a get out of prison free card—one with a high price tag.

Callie had been so out of it, so desperate, so fucking dope sick, she didn't care. She just wanted to get out of there and get high.

All the shame she felt that awful day nearly a year ago roared back. She'd left her mother alone, no one but strangers nearby, not even looking back once. At the time, two thoughts controlled her: freedom and pills.

Callie had sprinted all the way to the small, two-bedroom house her mother had been renting. After busting out a window, she'd grabbed a bag, loaded it down, and then raced to De'Shawn's house.

She'd begged him to help her since she hadn't snitched to the cops when she'd been arrested on campus. He agreed and took her to Memphis, in exchange for a hundred bucks and another blow job. Desperate to escape, high on the pills she'd bought from him with the cash stolen from her mother's hidden stash, she handed over the money—and her dignity.

Callie figured Memphis was a safe place to run. No one would ever look for her in a city and state miles from home where she knew no one.

It wasn't until they stopped at some filthy gas station before crossing the Mississippi River into Tennessee did she find out her mother had died. When she'd stepped into the station to use the bathroom and buy some water, it was the lead story on the news.

The lights inside her soul shut down.

The first two months in Memphis after De'Shawn dropped her off in a section of town that made downtown Little Rock look like Disneyland were terrifying. She'd spent most of her time bouncing from one seedy motel to another, searching for a job where she didn't have to fill out paperwork or provide ID. That proved to be impossible—even a job as a waitress required documentation. The grand she'd stolen from her mom went fast, and at the start of month three, Callie was on the streets.

Dirty, alone, and in need of a fix, Callie thought the cosmos finally cut her a break when a woman she'd later learn was named Teri

Cantrell strutted up to her, looking her up and down with dark, dead eyes. "You just gonna sit there and cry on that bench or use those legs and ass to make you some money?"

"Excuse me?"

"I said stop that crying and get to walking. Use what your mama gave you! If you don't do it on your own, someone you ain't gonna like will find you and *make* you."

Still young and somewhat naïve, Callie followed Teri home, grateful for a chance to sleep under a roof.

Shacking up with Teri turned out to be a bad decision.

A *really* bad decision.

Pills had made Callie numb to the world, but heroin turned Callie into a cold, heartless bitch.

The memories made her head spin. She tried to pray—her soul desperate for help—but the cravings were too intense to even utter one plea. The overwhelming desire to use consumed her mind. Callie's vision blurred, and she felt dizzy, unable to concentrate or form a clear sentence. The skin between her toes where the needle marks were hidden itched and burned. Callie's broken fingernails dug into the tender skin, scratching so hard she drew blood.

Collapsing to her knees, hands clasped over her ears, Callie rocked back and forth while mumbling the alphabet. "ABCDEF…" Over and over she chanted, first in only a breathy whisper. When that didn't work, she ramped up to yelling. By the third round, she was shrieking. *"ABCDEF…"*

"Stop all that racket or I'm calling the landlord!"

The gravelly voice of Randy Carlson, the obnoxious neighbor who lived in the unit next door, made Callie angry. He complained about the "shenanigans going on with those little whores in Unit B" all the time to the duplex's owner, Simon Greenwood, usually loud enough on the phone Callie heard him through the thin walls. Randy had no idea every single time he called to complain, Teri and Callie got a visit from Simon. He wouldn't say a word after letting himself inside the front door with his key. He'd just strip off all his clothes and wait for his needs to be met by either—or sometimes both—women.

Ignoring the blowhard despite her fears of the landlord finding out Teri was dead and possibly kicking her out, Callie continued. "ABCDEF…"

Bam! Bam! Bam!

Randy's meaty fists pounded on the wall. "I said shut up! I learned my ABCs a long time ago and don't need a refresher course! Jesus, just hurry up and smoke or shoot something. At least you're quiet when high. If you need cash, have Teri come over here. She's a better fuck than you are."

The words broke the last tendril of resolve. Sobbing, Callie scrambled to the bathroom, barely making it to the stained toilet before puking so hard stars appeared. Once finished, she stood and stared at the disheveled reflection looking back at her through the cracked mirror. A flicker of regret at seeing the gaunt, dirty woman with sunken cheeks, dark circles underneath dull eyes, and faded bruises and bumps, made her heart pound. Her nose hadn't healed right and now sported a strange knot at the bridge. Two of the cuts along her cheekbones should have had stitches and were going to leave ugly scars.

There wasn't even a trace of who she used to be. Not one bit. If anyone from her past were to walk by her now, they wouldn't even have a blip of recognition.

She didn't either.

Wiping away the flecks of vomit and a few straggler tears, Callie whispered. "Randy's right. I'm quiet when loaded. Everything is quiet when the venom enters the veins."

Grabbing her purse and phone from the counter, Callie stopped just shy of the door and turned around. On a whim, she grabbed her old backpack, stuffed it with the journal, photo album, and drawing pad. She feared returning home and finding herself locked out or robbed. Once the items were secured, she ran out the door and into the streets, heading toward the corner where she knew the white memory eraser awaited in the hands of countless dealers eager for their junkie clientele to arrive.

Callie ran toward her lover—her only real friend. Smack controlled her world, and she'd been stupid enough to think it would let her live without it. Heroin was a jealous bastard, unwilling to release her body from its death grip.

She found little comfort in the fact that at least this time, she had cash to pay for the smack, rather than turning a trick in exchange for a hit.

"I tried," Callie whispered to the cold night air, almost thankful she had no loved ones around to watch her crash and burn once again.

9

CHAPTER NINE

Later That Night

Spotting one of the dealers she frequented, Callie strode up to him. "Sable, I need some medicine real bad."

"Don't know what you mean, bitch. I ain't no—wait, KiKi? Is that you?"

Callie nodded, ignoring the shocked look on Sable's face.

"You look rough. Damn near didn't recognize you without your work clothes and makeup. Where you been?"

"Sable, please. No questions. I've got plenty of cash," Callie flashed the wad inside her wallet. "I'll take all you got."

Sable's eyes widened as he let out a low whistle. "No wonder I ain't seen you or Teri around. You two have been hitting a lot of johns! What's that, about eight hundred?"

Sweat poured down Callie's face. The shakes were making it hard to stand still. The bright lights and loud noises of the city made her feel dizzy. "Over a grand. Please, Sable. Help me."

"Dope sick's a bitch! If you want that much, baby, we need to take a walk. Follow me."

Relieved the pain would be gone soon, Callie followed Sable down the sidewalk. She'd buy enough to go out with a bang. Go home, fill the tub with hot water then slip away into the next life on a cloud of bliss. She didn't want to live any longer.

Not thinking straight as she planned out her exit strategy, Callie didn't notice they were in the dark alleyway where Teri died until it was too late. They were far away from the hubbub of the city—a hidden area rarely visited by people when darkness fell. Sable stopped walking and turned around. The smile on his face was the most terrifying thing she'd ever seen. "All of it. Now."

"Yes, all of it. How many grams will this get me?" Callie asked even though she knew Sable had no intention of selling her smack.

"You ain't getting shit. I'll be taking all you got," Sable hissed while snatching Callie's purse from her shoulder. Tossing it to the ground near his right leg, he stepped closer. "You recognize where you are, ho?"

The long, silver blade in his hand shimmered under the dim rays from a lone streetlight. Callie's blood ran cold. She lied. "Just an alley, Sable. Look, please, I need a fix! Take the money, I don't care, just leave me a few grams?"

Sable threw his head back, roaring with laughter. "Even only seconds away from the end, a junkie still wants a hit. You're pathetic. I'm ain't gonna make this easy for you. You're gonna die slow, in pain and alone, just like you let happen to Sugar Beets."

Taking a step back, Callie whispered, "I don't know what you're talking about."

"Lying bitch! You left her body and ran. She took you in, treated you like family—"

"Sable, please! Let me explain."

"Fuck you," Sable yelled, lunging forward.

Everything happened so fast Callie didn't have time to think about what she was doing. Primal instincts kicked in after the knife grazed her forearm, leaving a stinging gash. Ignoring the pain, Callie fought back like a wild woman, kicking and punching with all she had. Sable was smaller than she was but lightning fast. He caught her chin with a left hook, knocking her backward into the brick wall.

Seconds before, she was ready to end her life. She'd given up and wanted to die, yet now, the overwhelming urge to survive, to not have a dirty alley be the last thing she saw, fueled her limbs with renewed strength.

When Sable advanced, Callie tried to kick him in the knee, knowing if she did enough damage it would give her time to run. The oily, black pavement was slick from an earlier rain shower and she lost her balance, her foot barely grazing Sable's kneecap.

"Nice try, bitch!" Sable yelled.

She let out an ear-splitting scream as the knife plunged into her shoulder. Sable's body crushed hers against the wall.

Bombarded with pain, stunned by sheer terror, Callie stared into the dark, demented eyes of the last person she'd ever see while breathing. Sable crushed his lips on hers and whispered, "Rot in hell," while yanking the blade from her shoulder.

It took every ounce of strength Callie had not to collapse onto the ground. Blood soaked through the t-shirt, leaving traces of its warmth down her cold arm. Gasping for air as darkness crept in, Callie tried to force the dizziness away.

Time for my last stand she thought while making a fist. *God, I'm so sorry. For everything.*

Sable raised the knife, the gruesome, terrifying smile back. It disappeared when a noise to the right caught his attention.

"This ain't your business—" Sable grumbled.

"It is now."

Callie thought she was hallucinating. A man stepped out of the shadows and attacked Sable. She heard the sick sound of fleshing connecting with flesh. Sable never stood a chance as the man landed blow after blow, his huge hands covered in black gloves. The knife clattered across the pavement as Sable's body fell to the ground less than two feet away, blood seeping from the wounds to his face.

Shaking, mouth agape while staring at Sable's unmoving body, Callie looked for the rise and fall of his chest. Though slight, it was there. Shifting her attention back to the big man standing less than five feet away, she couldn't speak. Before she could blink twice, the stranger was by her side. He grabbed her free hand and pushed against the wound on her shoulder.

"Come on, we've got to get out of here. Keep pressure on it."

Close to fainting, Callie watched in silence as the man picked up her purse. He moved over to Sable's body, rifling through his pockets. After removing a wad of cash, he snatched up the knife. It disappeared into his pocket along with the money.

Her legs gave out. Callie slid down the wall, landing with a hard thump on the ground. Everything turned dark gray. She whispered, "Live. I want to live."

"Oh, shit. Come on girl, stay with me. We've got to get out of here."

"No hospital or cops. Take me to 4597 Hobson. B."

Callie couldn't utter another sound or see anymore. Darkness swallowed her up just as she felt her body being lifted. The wail of a distant siren made the stranger move faster.

"I've got you. Just hang on."

Opening her eyes, Callie winced as hot pain tore through her shoulder.

"Sorry. Sort of hoped you'd be out until I finished. Almost done."

Callie nodded while studying the face of the stranger tending to the wounds. His blond hair was in a buzz cut and deep, dark lines creased his face. He looked rough, dirty, and yet there was a hint of warmth behind his eyes. She'd never been good with guessing the age of others, but she thought he looked in his mid-forties. She was still too shaken up to really think straight, yet she searched her memories anyway. He didn't look familiar at all.

"There, all set. The shoulder and arm were only minor tissue damage. No nicks to any arteries or veins. I haven't patched anybody up like this in a long time and I'm a bit rusty, so the scars might be ugly later. Wish you'd change your mind about the hospital."

Unsure what to say, wary of the motivations of her rescuer, Callie stared at the makeshift bandage on her shoulder. It was the only clean bath towel she had. *Is this really happening? Maybe I'm still in the alley, half dead and hallucinating?*

"Afraid they'll discover your dirty secret?" the man asked while pointing at the track marks between Callie's toes.

Her mouth dropped open. "Who are you, and why did you help me?"

"Name's Mitchell."

Watching him grab the bloody towels and her clothes then step into the bathroom, Callie furrowed her brow. The man was dressed in black from head to toe, including dark smudges on his cheeks and forehead. She stole a quick glance around the bedroom, shocked to discover she was in her bed, naked. She pulled the dirty sheet over her body. "Got a last name, Mitchell? And an explanation of why you showed up like some avenging angel and saved my life?"

Chuckling while washing his hands, Mitchell responded, "I'm no angel. I just happened to be in the right place at the right time. Silly expression I know but in this case the truth."

Callie tried to sit up but a wave of dizziness made her stop. Her right arm throbbed. "Gee, thanks for clearing that up, and for undressing me. Was that really necessary?"

Mitchell flicked off the bathroom light, stepping back into the cramped bedroom. Without even asking, he removed his shoes and pants, turned off the overhead light, and then stretched out next to her on the bed. Callie's mouth went dry, wondering what fresh hell she'd woken up to and what was coming next.

After taking a deep breath, Mitchell said, "It was. Had to make sure I found all the wounds."

"Uh-huh," Callie muttered.

Silence fell between them for several minutes. The few rays of moonlight streaming in through the window helped her eyes adjust to the darkness. She wondered what time it was and how long she'd been out. Mitchell's breathing was deep and rhythmic. She hoped he'd fallen asleep.

"It's Sinclair. Nice to meet you, Ms. Novak."

"How did you—?" The question dried up in Callie's throat when Mitchell pointed to the backpack and purse on the floor. She couldn't hold her tongue any longer and let the questions fly. "Why did you help me? Why did you beat him up? Is he dead? Why did you bring me back here? Patch me up? Not insist I go to the hospital? Take the knife and his money? Please don't say you're hoping for free pussy for the rest of your life or other such nonsense like I'm your sex slave now. If that's the case, you should've just left me. I'm done with that life."

Chuckling softly, Mitchell answered, "You're a tough one. I'll give you that. Knew it when I saw you standing in the alley, all bloody and exhausted with your fist in the air. Sorry he got to you before I arrived. I lost him in the crowd. I followed the sound of your screams but was damn near too late. He's not dead, but when he wakes up, he'll probably wish he was. Sure would be nice to hear a thank you."

Callie's mind spun while attempting to make sense of the events of the last several hours. Was she really alive and back at Teri's? Did Sable really try to kill her and some random hero stepped in and beat his brains out? No, no way. She had to be dreaming, still plagued by strange nightmares from the withdrawals.

Part of her mind wanted to believe that, yet another whispered it was all real. Turning her head in his direction, she squinted in the darkness at Mitchell's massive, muscular back. She didn't get any sort of negative vibe from the man other than at some point, he'd either been a cop or perhaps in the military. The way he moved, spoke, and the wariness behind his eyes were dead giveaways. She'd serviced enough of the men in uniform to know. "Okay, Mitchell Sinclair. Thank you for saving me."

"Do you remember telling me you wanted to live?" Mitchell asked.

The memory was fuzzy but there. A smile tugged at the corners of her mouth because despite everything that happened, she did, which made absolutely no sense. What in the world did she have to live for or look forward to? She couldn't answer that question even inside her own mind, yet the will to continue on hummed in her chest. "Yes. I've got no clue how or where to start, but yes."

Rolling over to face her, Mitchell's blue eyes bored a hole into Callie's. "Do you mean it? You want to get off the shit and stop selling yourself on the streets? "

Raising an eyebrow, Callie asked, "Why do you care what I do with my life, Deputy Sinclair?"

"Detective Sinclair…retired. If you're going to be a smartass, you need to get it right."

"At least my cop radar still functions," Callie responded. "I didn't realize Shelby County cops turned into armed vigilantes when they retired. I mean, you're even wearing black for God sakes. Batman fetish?"

"Were you this mouthy before, or is this something new after the lowlife rang your bell?"

The teasing gleam behind Mitchell's eyes made Callie burst out laughing instead of responding with a witty retort about her own Dark Knight fantasies. Though the action made her arm throb, it felt wonderful to truly laugh. "I lost most of myself in the last year, but my smart mouth is one of the few things that remained."

"So, you're from Arkansas."

Callie stopped smiling as a tremor of worry skittered up her spine. Mitchell's words weren't said as a question—more like a statement of fact. She'd lost her driver's license months ago along with her social security card. The only way Mitchell could have known where she was from, along with her name, was by flipping through the photo album while she'd been unconscious. "Yeah, so?"

Propping up on an elbow, Mitchell said, "Me, too. I retired a few weeks ago after I lost my partner. I decided to make a trip to Memphis to release some inner demons."

She didn't like the direction the conversation was headed. "And you just happened to run into a fugitive from Little Rock in a dark alley getting jammed up by a drug dealer and then just for shits and giggles, intervene? No, wait, that's a silly question. I'm just dreaming. Any minute I'll wake up, run to the bathroom, puke my guts out, and realize my brain is totally fried."

"Let me guess. Day five of trying to quit on your own, you caved and went out searching to score?" Mitchell asked.

"Okay, now you're really starting to freak me out."

"Thought so. The first week is a fun ride on the paranoia train. Like I said earlier, you're a tough one. Five days clean on your own is rough and commendable. If you're serious about staying that way, I have connections. I could make some calls…get you into a treatment facility. That is, of course, if you're finished with the melodramatics?"

"Not possible. I don't have money or insurance. Am I finished freaking yet? Hardly. I'm just getting started."

Mitchell flopped back onto the pillow. "Okay, I give. Talk. Ask questions. Get it out of your system so I can rest. Then, once you stop yapping, I'll tell you what I can do for you."

Dumbstruck, Callie didn't know what to think. There was a sense of underlying danger, like he was hiding something from her, yet at the same time, Mitchell Sinclair reminded her of someone. It took a few minutes to figure out why she immediately took a shine to him and sensed she could trust him.

Daddy.

The man was tough, strong, brash, and cocky, yet he'd risked his life to save a complete stranger. Just like her father—a man who'd brought home countless stray animals over the years, determined to nurse them back to health—Mitchell seemed to want to help. Was it genuine?

Does it matter?

Taking a deep breath, grateful to have someone to talk to who was really listening without being judgmental or asking anything in return, Callie started her story.

She told him everything, starting with the horrible day on the track field up until Mitchell arrived in the alley. Talking helped keep her from thinking about drugs, for the most part. A few times, when the shakes and muscle cramps roared back, Mitchell gathered her into his arms, holding her close to his chest while stroking her hair until they passed. It was awkward and wonderful at the same time.

When she got to the part about De'Shawn, how he'd ambushed her in the bookstore parking lot, she felt Mitchell's muscles stiffen. When she broke down and sobbed after telling him what happened to her mother, his grip tightened as though he was trying to keep her from falling apart.

Hours passed and at some point, Callie finally ran out of words and fell into deep, restful sleep.

10

CHAPTER TEN

The Next Afternoon

It was late afternoon when she woke up to the sound of pots and pans clanging in the kitchen.

"Mitchell?"

He swore under his breath before answering. "Sorry. Never was any good at cooking. You ready for some ramen noodles and toast?"

"Actually, yes. I'm starving."

"Give me five," Mitchell called back.

Groaning as she exited the bed, Callie shuffled to the bathroom, stopping short when she caught her full reflection in the mirror. "Holy shit!"

"Yeah, those bruises will be really ugly by day three," Mitchell yelled. "Oh, and don't take a shower yet. Need that bandage on anther full day."

"Okay."

By the time she finished washing her face and gave herself a PTA bath, she heard Mitchell walk into the bedroom.

"Need some help getting dressed?"

"No, I'm fine," Callie answered while staring at a pair of red sweat pants and orange t-shirt draped over the towel rack. "You must be colorblind."

"Most men are," Mitchell answered. "Hurry up before the noodles get cold. They ain't great when warm, but when cold, it's like eating slimy worms."

Determined to take care of herself, Callie struggled to get dressed. By the time she finished, she was sweating.

When she walked into the small living area, she froze in the doorway. "Uh, what happened in here?"

Mitchell smirked, motioning for her to join him at the bar. "I needed something to do while you were sawing logs all afternoon."

"What did you do with all the junk?" Callie asked, gaze still focused on the clean living area.

"Bagged up most of it and took it to the dumpster out back. Had an interesting conversation with Randy."

Sitting down next to him, Callie said, "Randy's an asshole."

"I agree. And nosy. He asked one-too many questions. He's taking a nice, long nap now."

"Are you serious? You knocked him out? Why?"

Mitchell cast a sideways glance, arching one eyebrow. "Does it matter?"

"Guess not," Callie responded, studying Mitchell's face. "Did you really retire, or did you get kicked off the force? You know, for being too aggressive and refusing to take anger management classes or something? No, wait! You really aren't a cop. You're just on the run like I am. That makes more sense and explains why you stayed in this rat hole with a jonesing junkie."

"Again with the smart mouth. A full night's rest didn't help your attitude I see."

Callie set the spoon down and faced him. "Seriously, Mitchell. Why? Why were you following Sable last night? Why did you help me, clean up this nasty place, hold me while I cried and whined all night? I told you my tale of woe; now it's your turn."

Mitchell's jaw tightened as he stood. Reaching into his back pocket, he extracted his wallet. Flipping it open, he showed Callie his driver's license and the badge he'd received when he retired. "There, happy?"

"Okay, so you're really a retired detective named Mitchell Sinclair. That doesn't answer my other questions."

"There are some things better left unsaid, Callie. Everyone has secrets and a dark side. In the end, does the reason really matter how we found each other? Fate, divine intervention, karma, or the world's craziest twist of events. Call it what you like. For me, I'll take divine intervention. Now it's my turn to ask a question."

"Good Lord, what's left to know about me? You know more about me than my own mother did."

Mitchell stared at Callie for several seconds before answering. "You said last night you wanted to live and get clean. Still feel that way? I mean, are you truly ready to change your life?"

A lump of tears formed in her throat. Callie swallowed twice before answering, "Yes, but again, I don't have a clue where to start. I can't go back to Arkansas. It's too dangerous."

"Because you're worried about prison?"

"No, because of De'Shawn. Even here, he wouldn't leave me alone. About every three weeks he'd show up, demanding money to keep my whereabouts quiet. How he found me I have no clue, but he did. I'm stuck! If I go back, he'll find me, and if I stay, he'll find me. It's been about six weeks now, and when he comes by and I've got nothing to give him—"

"You don't need to worry about that. He won't be coming back. Ever."

"How do you know that?" Callie asked.

"Dead people can't travel."

The words slammed into Callie's mind like she'd been punched. "What?"

"Yep. Got his throat ripped out and most of his face eaten off by his dog, Hercules."

Stunned, Callie asked, "How do you know that?"

"Because I worked in the narcotics unit. De'Shawn was a narc. Answered to my partner."

The way Mitchell said the words made chills run up Callie's back. The look on his face, the raw anger, the quiet rage making his muscles tense, spoke volumes. She understood how De'Shawn found her—he knew Sable. Suddenly, it all made sense. Mitchell Sinclair had been hunting a drug dealer associated with De'Shawn. Why still wasn't clear, but she couldn't shake the sensation she was onto something.

Taking a deep breath, Callie finally asked, "So, I can really go home? I mean, I know I'll have to turn myself in and all, but a year in prison certainly can't be any worse than the year I've spent here."

Mitchell shook his head. "Rehab first and then we'll deal with the judicial system."

"We?" Callie whispered.

"Yeah, we. I've already made some calls this morning. When you're ready, I've got you a room for sixty days at *Brightwaters* in North Little Rock. When your arm heals enough to ride back with me, we'll go."

Tears raced down Callie's face while she stared at the man she'd only known for less than twenty-four hours. For the first time in three years, she had hope, and it showed up in a 6'4" bull of a man with a buzz cut and demons of his own.

Rising to her feet, Callie walked over to Mitchell, throwing her good arm around his burly neck. "Thank you for saving me, Mitchell. I mean it."

A look of intense sadness flashed across his face. Callie noticed a hint of tears glint in his eyes.

"The feeling's mutual."

She wondered exactly what he meant but decided now wasn't the time to ask. "Give me twenty minutes to pack, and we can go. I want to get out of here before the police show up asking questions about Sable."

"You didn't want to involve the police, so why in the world do you think a drug dealer would?"

Callie shrugged her shoulders. "Paranoia?"

Mitchell laughed. "I don't have a car, Callie. I rode a motorcycle. You really think you can handle 150 miles on the back with that arm?"

Callie glanced around the room, the place she'd sank to the lowest levels of her life and smiled. "Piece of cake, Dark Knight. Piece of cake. Let's roll."

"Dark Knight? Hmm, I've been called worse," Mitchell chuckled. "You realize the ride will be extremely uncomfortable and bumpy, right?"

Turning her gaze to Mitchell's inquisitive blue eyes, Callie knew his words weren't only about the actual drive to Arkansas. They were about the journey to sobriety she was embarking upon.

A race I started on my own. For me. Not for anyone else, but for me. I want this. I will do this. Like Coach Patterson used to say, I'll win this race for me.

"I think I'll be okay, Mitchell. If I start to wobble, I'll just hang on tighter."

11

EPILOGUE

Seven Months Later

"Great meeting, Regina. The speaker tonight was the best one yet!"

"She was good, wasn't she? Talk about God raising the dead!" Regina remarked while following Callie outside. "When are you going to start doing the same?"

Callie laughed. "Uh, never. Public speaking isn't my thing. I'd fall apart. I'm still struggling to deal with what I went through with you, and you're my sponsor. The thought of standing up in front of a room full of others terrifies me."

"You'll do it. I know you will. I've never been wrong before. God will let you know when you're ready."

Callie blushed. "I still struggle with the whole higher power thing, Regina. I mean, I grew up in church and all, yet we quit going when my grandparents died. I'm not sure I'll know if he's leading me to do anything."

Regina waved her hands in the air. "Doesn't matter. He'll know, just like he knew you were ready to go visit the graves of your family to say goodbye two weeks ago."

Callie shuddered at the memory of the painful day. "I guess."

"So, new topic. How's the job?"

"I love it. I mean, why wouldn't I? I get to see animals all day long. It's kind of a bummer when one comes in sick, but when just for a checkup or shots, it's a blast. Dr. Sinclair is so kind. He knows I can't have pets so last week, the office officially adopted the cutest cat someone dumped off. Big, orange and white tabby we named

Sherbert. He spends the majority of his days sleeping right next to the computer."

Regina smiled. "Good to hear. I knew you'd be a good fit in his office."

"Thank you again for recommending me. Dr. Sinclair's a really nice man. He told me if things go sour tomorrow, I'd still have a job when I get out. Isn't that sweet?"

"It is," Regina replied. She put her hand on Callie's arm. "Don't stress about court tomorrow, Callie. God's got this. You've come a long way in seven months."

"I know," Callie sighed. She'd been fighting off the worry about appearing in court. "You're going to be there, right?"

"Wouldn't miss it!" Regina answered while scouring the parking lot. "You need a ride?"

The roar of Mitchell's motorcycle pulling into the parking lot drowned out Callie's response.

"Oh, guess not. Hunky McHunk is here. I still can't believe you two are just friends. Come on, spill. It's just us girls. What's really going on between the two of you? I've never seen someone who wasn't a family member come to visit a client every single Friday."

"We're just really close. That's all. We get each other."

Regina licked her lips as Mitchell parked the bike. "I'd like to get me some—"

"Sounds like someone needs a cold shower or a bucket of ice dumped on them," Callie said, shaking her head. Regina was practically drooling. "The man's old enough to be my father and yours."

"Oh, Daddy, I've been really bad."

Holding up her hand, Callie interrupted. "Okay, enough. I get it. See you next week."

Turning, Callie walked away, leaving her sponsor alone with her sick fantasies about Mitchell.

"So, how was the meeting?" Mitchell asked.

Climbing on to the back of the bike, she answered, "Good. The speaker's testimony was amazing. The woman endured horrors way worse than mine. She's an inspiration."

"So are you. Come on, I want to take you somewhere I think you're ready to see. Gotta hurry before curfew at the house."

"Last night, the house mother went off on Charlotte, the girl who arrived earlier in the week. She found a baggie of meth and then all hell broke loose. It was crazy and intense for about thirty minutes."

"Can't blame her. It's not called a chemfree house for nothing."

"So, where are we going?"

"You'll see. Helmet, please."

Callie didn't argue. She loved riding with Mitchell. It gave her a sense of freedom and a rush. Wrapping her arms around his waist, she sighed. She would never admit it to anyone, but she did have a slight crush on him, which made sense. He'd saved her life—been her Dark Knight swooping in to rescue her—but that's as far as she'd let it go.

She wouldn't let anyone stand in her way of staying sober and working on herself. There would be no point. Right now, she wouldn't be able to offer anything to a relationship anyway, and though she was attracted to Mitchell on certain levels, the thought of getting intimate with anyone made her stomach twist into a knot. After what she'd experienced in Memphis, sex was the last thing on her mind.

Sometimes at night when she couldn't sleep, she considered trying to contact Kevin. In the end, she decided too much had happened, too much time had passed, and it was time to let go. The last conversation they had when he came over and helped Callie and her mother pack and move had been awkward and strained. Kevin's life plans never included having a junkie as his mate. Though clean and sober now, she knew the rest of her life would be a struggle to remain that way, and she refused to drag Kevin into the mess. His heart had already been destroyed once. Every time Callie thought about the look on his face graduation night—the words "I'm willing to break my own heart to fix yours"—she'd tear up.

She wouldn't risk hurting him again. He'd always hold a special place inside her heart, but he deserved to have a woman who wasn't so damaged.

"Here we are."

Callie removed the helmet and stared at the beautiful place. A small ranch house surrounded by tall trees and a white picket fence sat in front of them. Stretching around the side of the house was fresh concrete and the bare bones of a building. "Is this your place?"

"No, but I'll be living here soon, once the construction on the apartments is completed."

Curious after noticing a small wooden sign that read *The Joshua Tree* tacked to the front gate, Callie asked, "What kind of place is this?"

"Come on, I'll show you."

They climbed off the bike and walked around back. A large pond with several weeping willows hanging over it looked like it was on fire as the last rays of the sun caressed the top of the water. "Oh, this is beautiful! Any fish in there?"

Pointing to a small bench ahead, Mitchell answered, "Not yet, but that's another item on the agenda. Fishing is relaxing, and addicts need all of that they can get."

"Addicts? This place will be a treatment facility?"

"That's the plan. We'll have housing for about twenty at a time. Once I finish the buildings, the next project is a walking trail that leads to an old barn back there." Mitchell pointed to a large clump of trees. "Going to add a big gazebo next to the pond so people can meditate."

"So why did you bring me here? I've already gone through rehab and been living in chemfree housing for months."

Mitchell let the normal edginess he wore like an accessory drop. "Do you remember when you thanked me for saving you and I said the feeling's mutual?"

"Yes."

"I wasn't kidding. Let me tell you why I was in Memphis."

"Okay."

"This place was owned by an amazing woman named Merry Hall. She left it all to her best friend, Debbie, who lives here and has been helping me set this all up. You see, Merry's son, Joshua, was murdered during a drug deal. At his funeral, Merry's husband, Harold, suffered a massive heart attack and died. It left the poor woman so broken she died less than six months later."

Callie gasped. "Dear God, how awful!"

"Merry's brother, Derek, was my partner. We went to the academy together. He was the closest thing to a brother I've ever known. The last six years we worked together in the narcotics unit. Derek was De'Shawn's handler. I would have given up my life for Derek. I trusted him that much. Unfortunately, he let the life lure him in. Joshua witnessed a deal go down between his uncle and De'Shawn, and Derek killed him, making it look like he overdosed on heroin. Not long after, Derek was shot during a deal. He didn't survive."

Callie's eyes widened in shock as everything clicked. "Oh, Mitchell, I'm so sorry. You wanted revenge, didn't you? Is that why you went to Memphis? Looking for De'Shawn?"

Mitchell's jaw tightened. He wouldn't look Callie in the face. "No. De'Shawn was already dead. I went to find the next rung in the ladder—the guy Derek had been buying from. He'd been making runs to Memphis, and when I realized why, I decided to go find the piece of shit he'd been buying from and kill him. That person was Sable."

"But you didn't kill him! You saved me instead."

Turning to face her, Mitchell whispered. "If you wouldn't have been there, I would have crossed a line I'm not sure I could ever come back from."

Unsure what to say, Callie simply leaned closer and hugged Mitchell with all her strength. They sat together on the bench for several minutes, each clinging to the other like lost siblings. Finally, Callie asked, "So that's why it's named *The Joshua Tree.* What a lovely gesture."

"The night I found you, I felt something change inside me. Like I said back then, I believe it was divine intervention. I knew taking the life of just one pathetic dealer wouldn't help people like you. What will help is a place they can go and have more than just a detox experience. I had a lot of long conversations with Debbie, and we came up with this plan. I needed to change my focus, let the anger go, and do something positive with my life. This place will be for healing the mind, body, and soul. And I'd like you to be a part of it as a counselor."

Callie's mouth dropped open. "Come again?"

"If you want to, of course. Completely up to you, but the offer is on the table. You would be a great counselor and could help others. Helping others, and yourself in the process, will give those ruined wings on your foot a chance to soar."

"Oh, Mitchell. I don't know what to say. I'm honored and terrified at the same time. Will the offer still be available when I get out of prison? You know, after I go before the judge tomorrow?"

Mitchell stood, swiping his hand across his face to rid it of his tears. "If you agree to come work here, stay drug free and submit to random testing, attend drug counselor classes, and graduate, then you'll be on probation for three years under my watchful eye. Worked the deal out myself with the prosecutor and the judge today."

Callie burst into tears. So much had happened in four years. Complete strangers stepped in and changed her life. A hint of worry about whether she could maintain her sobriety made her shiver. "I can't believe this. You really are an angel sent from above."

Mitchell put his arms around Callie, pulling her to his chest. "The feeling's mutual, CeeCee."

About the Author

Award-winning and International bestselling author, Ashley Fontainne, is an avid reader of mostly the classics. Ashley became a fan of the written word in her youth, starting with the Nancy Drew mystery series. Stories that immerse the reader deep into the human psyche and the monsters lurking within us are her favorite reads.

Her muse for penning the *Eviscerating the Snake* series was *The Count of Monte Cristo* by Alexandre Dumas. Ashley's love for this book is what sparked her desire to write her debut novel, *Accountable to None*, the first book in the trilogy. With a modern setting to the tale, Ashley delves into just what lengths a person is willing to go to when they seek personal justice for heinous acts perpetrated upon them. The second novel in the series, *Zero Balance,* focuses on the cost and reciprocal cycle that obtaining revenge has on the seeker. Once the cycle starts, where does it end? How far will the tendrils of revenge expand? *Adjusting Journal Entries* answered that question—far and wide.

The short thriller entitled *Number Seventy-Five*, touches upon the sometimes dangerous world of online dating. *Number Seventy-Five* took home the BRONZE medal in fiction/suspense at the 2013 Readers' Favorite International Book Awards contest and is currently in production for a feature film.

The paranormal thriller entitled *The Lie*, won the GOLD medal in the 2013 Illumination Book Awards for fiction/suspense and is also in production for a feature film entitled *Foreseen*.

Ashley decided to delve into the paranormal with a Southern Gothic horror/suspense novel, *Growl*, which released in January of 2015. The suspenseful mystery, *Empty Shell*, released in September of 2014. Ashley teamed up with Lillian Hansen (Ashley calls her mom!) and penned a three-part murder mystery/suspense series entitled *The Magnolia Series*. The first book, *Blood Ties*, released in 2015, and was voted one of the Top 50 Self-Published Books You Should Be Reading in 2015 at www.readfree.ly.

Whispered Pain released in October of 2015 and *Night Court* released December 13, 2015.

Tainted Cure, Tainted Reality, and *Tainted Future* are the first three books in the post-apocalyptic/zombie genre, *The Rememdium Series,* all released in 2016 to rave reviews for a fresh take on the zombie genre.

Connect with Ashley:

Website: http://www.ashleyfontainne.com – Sign up for Ashley's newsletter and receive a free ebook!

Twitter: https://twitter.com/ashleyfontainne

Facebook: https://www.facebook.com/ashley.fontainne

Movie site: http://www.foreseenmovie.com

www.ingramcontent.com/pod-product-compliance
Lightning Source LLC
Chambersburg PA
CBHW020547310726
48979CB00008B/1123/J

* 9 7 8 0 9 9 6 0 1 7 9 5 4 *